DISTANT THUNDER

The Wakefield family spend their first holiday abroad in Brussels, which proves to be a bad choice in the summer of 1815.

As battle erupts unexpectedly the Wakefields are unable to flee and are caught up in a series of mysteries in addition to the perils of a country at war.

A jewel theft, an abduction, the discovery of a dead body in the park and the disappearance and possible murder of a young officer all follow in quick succession.

The story is told by Elizabeth Aston, the Wakefields' niece. Although occupied with care of the wounded she starts an investigation with the help of a Bow Street Runner. She finds love and danger on the way.

'Sunday came, and the battle, about nine miles off, began to roar. It was described by the inhabitants of Brussels as one uninterrupted peal of thunder in their ears for ten hours.'

James Simpson

'We became sensible of a dull, sullen sound that filled the air, somewhat resembling . . . distant thunder.'

Captain Cavalié Mercer

DISTANT THUNDER

Rosemary Craddock

ARTHUR H. STOCKWELL LTD
Torrs Park, Ilfracombe, Devon, EX34 8BA
Established 1898
www.ahstockwell.co.uk

British Library Cataloguing-in-Publication Data.
A catalogue record for this book is available
from the British Library.

By the same author
The Secret House (Robert Hale Ltd)
The Abbey Governess (Robert Hale Ltd)
Templewood (Robert Hale Ltd)
The Dark City (Robert Hale Ltd)
Surgeons' Square (Robert Hale Ltd)
The Crooked Street (Robert Hale Ltd)
Devil's Folly (Robert Hale Ltd)
The Lovegrove Hermit (Robert Hale Ltd)
Avalon Castle (Robert Hale Ltd)

ISBN 978-0-7223-4847-5
Printed in Great Britain by
Arthur H. Stockwell Ltd
Torrs Park   Ilfracombe
Devon EX34 8BA

CHAPTER ONE

My cousin Benjamin and I had never liked each other. This antipathy began in childhood when, after the death of my parents, I came to live in Birmingham with my Uncle Nat and Aunt Hetty. Ben and I were nearly the same age; his sister Carrie was born later, so he was the spoilt only son of the family and greatly resented the intrusion of another child, a mere girl at that, who was little more than a stranger.

He was forever pulling my hair, kicking my shins and stealing my toys, though never when there was an adult about. When he broke his hobby horse after losing his temper and hurling it against the wall, he blamed me and I was punished.

My Uncle Nat was usually fair in his judgements, but he was occupied with the prosperous family jewellery business so it was Aunt Hetty who was left to deal with the children. She was kind enough, especially at first, when she called me a poor motherless lamb, but 'Benjie', as she insisted on naming him, always came first. I accepted this as I accepted everything else in the way children do, but I was relieved when he was sent to school.

Not a boarding school! Aunt Hetty thought him too delicate for that and too sensitive in disposition to be taken away from her. King Edward's Grammar School probably contained rude, rough boys who would make his life a misery or coarsen him irrevocably. So Ben was sent to a small local school, which was run, quite ineffectively, by an elderly clergyman.

He grew into a bully, arrogant and conceited but barely literate. He scarcely spoke to me save to sneer at the uselessness and stupidity of girls. Occasionally I hit back. When he called me

'Gipsy' on account of the dark colouring I had inherited from an Italian grandmother, I retorted with 'Carrot Head', which made him very angry indeed, to my great delight. His red hair was not really carroty at all, but he was very sensitive about it. This was the only sensitivity he ever seemed to show.

By this time his little sister, Carrie, six years younger, was beginning to make her presence felt. She had a temper equal to his, which did not prevent her from becoming her father's darling.

Uncle Nat hoped Ben would join him in the family business, but he considered that demeaning and boring. He tried several other occupations, but none of them seemed to suit. First he studied the law, but found it tedious; then he went into banking, but he had to begin as a clerk and that was beneath him. At last he joined the militia and could swagger around in a uniform, but that was not quite dashing enough so he transferred to the regular army, much to Aunt Hetty's distress.

By now he had grown into a handsome young man with curly red-gold hair. 'Like an angel!' declared his doting mother. He also had a winning but totally misleading smile.

My aunt was greatly relieved when peace was made with France and Bonaparte exiled to Elba. This occurred shortly after Ben bought his commission in a serving regiment. The real trouble began when the late emperor escaped and returned to France. As Britain took up arms again, Lieutenant Benjamin Wakefield was ordered to Belgium.

'I must go with him!' cried Aunt Hetty. 'Everyone says there will be a great battle against Bonaparte himself. Suppose Ben is wounded – who will look after him?'

'Our army intends to invade France. We're not going to follow him there,' said my uncle.

'We may be able to when Boney is defeated.'

'We'll see about that when the time comes.'

Uncle Nat was so used to his wife's wild outbursts that he encountered them with amused tranquillity. He refused at first to consider any possibility of going abroad. Then several events followed in quick succession which made him change his mind.

We had always shared a large house on Summer Hill with

Uncle Nat's brother Josiah, who was the senior partner in the family business.

It stood on the borders of the jewellery quarter. Josiah, a gloomy, taciturn man who had been widowed early in life, occupied a whole floor with his equally solemn and silent son, Jacob. The latter ran a prosperous jewellery shop in Corporation Street. Josiah, however, wished to expand the business. He and Uncle Nat decided to venture into a more fashionable area and fixed on Bath as most suitable.

A property was found and alterations were under way to prepare the shop and its workrooms and living quarters for Uncle Nat, a couple of craftsmen and the rest of the family. The great move was planned and the Summer Hill house rented out as Josiah and Jacob moved to smaller accommodation.

There was some talk of a holiday before the new business was ready, but nothing had been decided when a problem arose. Carrie was now a pretty, flighty girl of seventeen. She was sent off to stay with an uncle and aunt in London. Aunt Hetty's brother Daniel was a prosperous apothecary and had connections with the leading surgeons of the capital. Surgeons, however, had medical students and somehow one of them took a fancy to Carrie, and she to him. They attempted an elopement, were caught in the act and it was decided that Carrie must immediately be removed as far as possible from the young man's influence.

Aunt Hetty was eager to go to Brussels to be near her beloved Benjie. Hundreds of British people were flocking there, delighted to cross the Channel after so many years of isolation. One of Ben's superior officers secured rooms for us in a respectable hotel where my cousin was billeted, and we were assured that the city was perfectly safe, especially now that the Duke of Wellington had arrived. It was expected that the army would set out to confront Bonaparte in France sometime around the 20th of June. Meanwhile everyone was enjoying a delightful, carefree holiday in the most festive city in Europe.

Even Carrie cheered up at the prospect of all those dashing uniforms. We set out in high spirits, unaware that our troubles were just beginning.

CHAPTER TWO

As none of us had ever been abroad before we had no idea of the possible horrors of a sea crossing. We began the journey happily enough, but were soon overwhelmed by a nightmare of noise, motion, seasickness and chaos. The packet boat was crowded with passengers: travellers, soldiers, servants and horses. My aunt went below with Carrie and a Mrs Moffat to groan away the thirty hours of our unfortunate passage. I stayed on deck with my uncle, preferring the fresh air and sea spray to the stifling stench of the nether regions. We were much obliged to a couple of officers who were very kind and concerned for our comfort. There was also a great deal of attention – perhaps too much – from Mr Moffat.

We had met the Moffats the night before we set sail at the Albion Hotel, Ramsgate. As soon as they discovered we were all bound for the Hôtel Britannique in Brussels they offered instant friendship. Carrie promptly christened them 'the Spratts'. They certainly bore some resemblance to the pair in the nursery rhyme as Mr Moffat was thin and his wife was fat, though whether this was due to their diet we had no idea.

Mr Moffat was by no means an ill-looking man, though a little below average height and bespectacled, with colourless straight hair. Yet he was neat to the point of being dapper and his bright cornflower-blue eyes twinkled behind his steel-rimmed spectacles. He was very amiable, garrulous and cheerful; I thought him a harmless busybody as he seemed well informed about our fellow passengers, the situation in Belgium and even Bonaparte's actions in France.

'We are often given misleading information,' he declared, 'sometimes deliberately. I must know the truth. I am looking forward to our sojourn in Brussels, at the very centre of everything that is going on. You have a son in the army, I understand?' He turned to Uncle Nat.

'Yes, he helped us to obtain accommodation. I understand Brussels is crowded with English visitors.'

'So I believe. We have no military connections, but I was anxious to get my wife away from England. I thought a sojourn in another country could do her good. I'm sorry to say she was a devotee of the late Joanna Southcott.'

'The prophetess?' I exclaimed.

'The bogus prophetess. She led many astray with her idiotic pronouncements. And then – would you believe it? – she claimed to be bearing the new Messiah – at over sixty! It turned out to be a dropsy of course and she died. Poor Phoebe was very distressed; all her illusions were shattered. I don't think she's quite got over it, even now.'

'I'm sure the excitement of a foreign tour will do her good,' I said, wishing he would be quiet or go away as I was beginning to feel queasy. I stood up and the deck heaved beneath my feet and I lost my balance. Mr Moffat threw out a supporting arm and helped me to sit down again. 'Try to keep absolutely still,' he advised.

'Still? Nothing is still. I don't feel at all well.'

At that moment my poor uncle, who had turned quite green, staggered to the side of the ship. Mr Moffat ran after him.

'Not that side, my good sir! The wind will blow in your face and all will fly back at you. The other side – I will assist you.'

I was overwhelmed by a wish to be horizontal and decided to brave the lower regions. A middle-aged man who was sitting by the companionway wrapped in a boat-cloak suddenly sprang into life and offered help, for which I was most grateful.

'Do you know that man?' he asked.

'Mr Moffat? No, we met him at Ramsgate. He introduced himself. He seems very affable.'

'Oh yes, he's that all right! Now you go and lie down and hope the sea turns calm. I'll tell your father.'

I did not bother to correct him, but took his advice. As he was rather nondescript despite a distinct Cockney accent, I doubted if I would recognise him if I ever saw him again.

The rest of the voyage passed like a nightmare from which it was impossible to awaken. The situation below was just as horrible as I expected, but once in my berth nothing on earth would have persuaded me to leave it.

Ostend was reached at last and I remained very shaky for some time, partly from sickness but also from the fact that I had been unable to eat anything since we began the crossing. The two officers were a great help and threatened some obstructive officials with being 'reported to the Duke' if they impeded the progress of honest English travellers.

The town seemed mean and dirty, but we were directed to a comfortable inn where I was able to enjoy a good meal. Never had a bed seemed more welcome and I fell instantly asleep.

We resumed our journey on the morrow and travelled to Bruges, where we spent two days, and then, by a large and comfortable canal boat, to Ghent. Again we stayed to see the sights before travelling by hired carriage along a well-paved road to Brussels. By now we were in high spirits and enjoying the journey, looking out on the peaceful, prosperous countryside. The Moffats, who had stayed close to us during the last few days, travelled in another carriage behind, which they shared with two other English travellers.

'Mrs Moffat told me her husband was a lawyer,' said my aunt. 'I'm not sure what sort, but he dealt principally with wills. Then he inherited some money, enough to give up work and see something of the world. They live in London – I can't remember where, but they seem very respectable.'

'He's a bit of a know-all,' said Uncle Nat, 'but well informed. He says our army will invade France about the 20th of June.'

'That's what Benjie told us in his letter. That means we'll have at least five or six weeks with him. I'm *so* looking forward to seeing him again. He must miss the comforts of home.'

'Well, he couldn't have been posted anywhere more comfortable than here. He's staying in our hotel and doing very well for himself as far as I can tell.'

We approached Brussels at sunset and suddenly witnessed a scene that sent a chill through me. A long line of mounted troops rode slowly past us. They were all dressed in black, their shakos crowned with black plumes and ornamented with a silver skull and crossbones. Their horses were as black as themselves. The immediate impression was of a funeral procession.

'The Black Brunswickers,' my uncle explained. 'Moffat told me about them. They wear mourning for the death of their duke. The present duke is their commander.'

'How dismal!' exclaimed Aunt Hetty. 'I'm so glad our Benjie wears scarlet. It's much more cheerful and becoming.'

I said nothing, but thought that was just the silly sort of remark I would expect my aunt to make.

Carrie seemed interested in the troopers. 'How romantic! ' she sighed.

We passed through the lower part of the town, where the streets were narrow and mean, dark already in the twilight, and came to the higher town, which was light and airy with elegant shops and an atmosphere of liveliness and bustle. After driving through the vast Place Royale with its handsome classical buildings, we turned into a quiet residential street near the park and arrived at our destination, the Hôtel Britannique.

The proprietor and his wife came out to meet us and welcomed us in English. I soon discovered that Monsieur Dubois spoke the language well, though with a heavy accent. His wife spoke it perfectly, having been brought up in London. I think we all found this a comfort. My uncle spoke no French, my aunt and cousin very little, and I knew enough to get by reasonably well.

My aunt's pleasure was at once mitigated by the information that we were on the third floor and we had to climb a hundred stone steps to reach our rooms.

'Accommodation is very hard to obtain,' explained Madame

Dubois. 'We are full of officers. When the invasion of France begins we will have plenty of room and you can all move down.'

My aunt was not pacified. A hundred steps brought on the vapours, to say nothing of her 'bad back', which provided her with an excuse for avoiding anything she did not wish to do.

Somehow we got her upstairs. On each landing was a window seat set in an embrasure, where she was able to rest for a few minutes. We had nothing to carry save a few light bags as our heavier luggage was being brought up by the hotel servants.

Suddenly, while my aunt was gasping on the second landing, there was a great clattering on the stairs and Ben came running down to meet us.

'I thought it was you!' he cried. 'Welcome to Brussels! I'm afraid we're a bit crowded here and I'm sharing with two others, but your rooms are very decent. How are you, Mama?'

He submitted to her tears and embraces with a good grace, shook hands with his father and bestowed a perfunctory peck on Carrie and me. Then he helped Aunt Hetty up the remaining stairs, and somehow she forgot her weariness and questioned him unendingly about his diet and general comfort.

'Well, girls,' said Uncle Nat, 'we'll have to take second place from now on, it seems. Up we go! I wonder how the Moffats contrived a room on the first floor? I suppose they reserved it before we did.'

Ben, my aunt was delighted to discover, was in a room at the other end of our corridor. There were no private sitting rooms in the hotel, only bedrooms. These were all very clean and well appointed and provided with small tables and chairs in case guests wished to take meals in their rooms. My aunt took advantage of this arrangement and had supper sent up to her. Ben stayed with her and no doubt much gossip and affection was exchanged during the evening. Carrie and I felt excluded and retired to our room next door, where Molly, our maid, helped us to unpack.

Next morning Aunt Hetty declared that she needed more time to recover from the journey. The rest of us could go forth and explore Brussels. She was sure we could all walk further than she was able and secure tickets for any amusements that might be available.

Ben, whose military duties seemed very light, offered to accompany us as our guide; and we were joined by Mr Moffat, who told us his wife was spending the morning in bed, quite exhausted by the exertions of the last few days.

I was ready before the others and waiting by the door into the street, watching the passers-by. Soon I became aware of a man I vaguely recognised, lounging on the other side of the road smoking a pipe. On seeing me he knocked out his pipe, waved and came over to me. I realised it was the man who had helped me below deck on the boat. At close quarters in a good light I revised my opinion of his appearance. There was nothing unusual about him apart from a certain sharpness of feature and a keen, alert expression. He was not a gentleman but neat, presentable and quite respectable. I could not place him at all.

'Good morning, Miss Aston. I trust you are feeling better now.'

'Of course, but—'

'I was privileged to offer you a small assistance at sea.'

'Yes indeed, I was most grateful. But you know my name?'

'Ah, I make it my business to know everybody.'

I was tempted to ask, 'What *is* your business?' but thought it might appear rude.

'Are you staying here?' I enquired instead.

'Not in this hotel. I have lodgings down the street. Clean and comfortable, but the landlady is a terror. She will not have smoking in the house. She's had a clutch of hulking great Highlanders billeted on her and they behave like meek little lambs and take their pipes outside.'

At that moment we were interrupted by a thickset, broad-shouldered man, rather shabbily dressed, who edged his way past us rather impolitely, muttering something beneath his breath, whether excuse or curse I could not tell.

'Do you know who that is?' enquired my companion.

'I've only see him once before, but I've only just arrived.'

'He's in a little attic on the top floor with the landlady's broken furniture. He used to be a naval surgeon, but something went wrong.'

'A lot of naval men are on half-pay since the war ended. No one knew it would start up again.'

'Ah, there's more to it than that. He has an interesting past.' He broke off suddenly, glancing over my shoulder. 'I must go, Miss Aston. I expect we both have much to do and see this morning.'

'Yes indeed, we—'

But he was gone. I realised that although he knew my name I still did not know his.

I was glad my aunt was not with us as she would undoubtedly have slowed our progress. As it was, we walked to the point of exhaustion, though I was not aware of my weariness until our return. Ben rattled nineteen to the dozen, though Mr Moffat bade fair to rival him. Ben, however, knew the city, and we were able to secure seats for the theatre and opera and tickets for a public ball at the Hôtel de Ville.

The atmosphere in the city was light-hearted to the point of frivolity, as though everyone was bent on pleasure. There were many English visitors – around 1,500 according to Mr Moffat, without counting the soldiers. The 5th Division, which included Ben's regiment, was the only one stationed in Brussels itself, but many officers came in from the surrounding area in search of amusement. War seemed to be the last thing on anyone's mind, although uniforms were everywhere: some foreign, but mostly the scarlet of the British Army, with the blue of the Artillery and Hussars and the dark green of the Rifles. All seemed to be smiling and laughing and some saluted Carrie, who was wide-eyed with delight.

We visited the park last, as it was on the way back to our hotel and there were seats where we could rest and watch the world go by. The park was the hub of life in Brussels. No horses were allowed within its extensive boundaries, so everyone was on foot. The gravel pathways were crowded with elegantly dressed ladies in light pelisses with parasols, many on the arms of officers, strolling under the trees. There were many formal walks with statues and fountains, a lake and a pavilion selling refreshments. Some areas were more natural, with thick shrubberies, winding paths and pretty little dells.

As we sat comfortably watching the passers-by, something odd happened. I saw two ladies walking in our direction. One was a handsome woman of forty or so and very elegantly and expensively dressed. Her companion was much younger, and from a certain facial resemblance I thought she must be the lady's daughter.

Mr Moffat immediately sprang to his feet and approached her with outstretched hand. She recoiled slightly and seemed reluctant to take it, but then allowed him to press her hand and, quite unnecessarily, raise it to his lips. He spoke to her for a few minutes, which gave me time to study her attire and jewellery, which were in perfect taste for the time of day. Then she walked on, a curious expression on her face which I could not quite fathom.

Mr Moffat came back, rubbing his hands together in glee.

'That was Lady Silbury,' he explained, 'one of my former clients. I dealt with her husband's will a while back. Rather my speciality, wills. At all events she has asked me to call on her at the Hôtel Belle Vue in one hour.'

In Brussels dinner was taken between three and four o'clock, which seemed very strange to us, but we soon grew used to it. On this afternoon Mrs Moffat turned up quite smartly attired and I noticed she was wearing a large cameo brooch which seemed strangely familiar. It was very like the one worn by Lady Silbury that morning. I could have been wrong; I had not been close enough to Her Ladyship to take in details, but I had noticed that the cameo bore a male head, which was rather uncommon. I thought it was the Apollo Belvedere. Then I realised what Lady Silbury's expression had been. It was fear.

CHAPTER THREE

We soon came to know the other guests in the hotel. I do not include the officers, who were coming and going, clanking and clattering all hours of the day and night. They laughed a great deal and seemed not to have a care in the world, though most of them had experience of war.

'Don't worry about Boney, dear lady,' one of them assured me when we met on the stairs one day. 'We'll give him a good licking. He's never faced the Duke. In the meantime, eat, drink and be merry—'

'For tomorrow we die!' added a lugubrious voice over his shoulder.

The speaker, despite his mournful tone, was laughing and I recognised a handsome, curly-haired young officer of the Rifles who shared a room with his brother on the same floor as me.

'Oh, you sweeps! ' grinned the scarlet-coated lieutenant before me. 'Take no notice of anyone in green, ma'am. They lurk in the undergrowth where no one can see them and shoot everything that moves.'

At that moment a very young man in an ensign's uniform came hurtling past us, sketching a salute, and rushed downstairs with a great clatter.

'Slow down, you young rogue, or you'll save the French the expense of a bullet,' his superior officer yelled after him.

'You must excuse him,' said the Lieutenant. 'He's new to the army and in for a shock one day, but he's so keen I don't like to discourage him.'

'He doesn't look old enough to be in the army,' I observed.

'He's only sixteen – straight from school.'

'Hayward!' called a youthful voice from below. 'Are you coming down, sir?'

'I must obey,' said the lieutenant. 'Young Parker has spoken. I hope to see you again, ma'am.'

He went on his way, leaving me alone with the Rifles officer.

'Why did he call you sweeps?' I asked.

'Oh, it's a nickname the inferior part of the army gives us on account of our dark uniforms. They're stuck with the old red rag, of course, and fire muskets and carry colours and form squares to receive cavalry. We don't do any of that.'

'You lurk?'

'You might say that, but it's all to a purpose as I hope to explain to you sometime. But disparaging remarks are usually prompted by envy. Everybody knows we're the best regiment in the army.'

'I wouldn't dare to dispute it.'

'But I haven't introduced myself. Charles Croft at your service.'

'Don't you share a room with your brother along the corridor from us?'

'Yes, we came over with my regiment; we landed on the 27th of April. Henry came on ahead to secure a room for us. He found an English horse dealer in Ostend and bought us some useful nags. They're a lot cheaper here.'

'You don't know who I am,' I said, feeling at a disadvantage.

'Oh, but I do. I took the trouble to find out. You are Miss Elizabeth Wakefield and your brother is sharing a room with Hayward and Parker, who have just left us.'

'Then you are misinformed. My surname is Aston and Lieutenant Wakefield is my cousin, not my brother. I am travelling with my uncle and aunt.'

'That explains it! You don't look like any of them. May I ask if you are enjoying the amusements of Brussels?'

'Very much. It's like being part of some grand fête. We are going to the theatre, the opera and a public ball at the Hôtel de Ville.'

'Ah, I may see you there. It'll be one of the Belgian balls – a bit staid, you know – they finish at one in the morning. The

17

other balls are given by very grand people. My brother and I get an occasional invitation, but we can't afford to accept. We don't belong in that sort of society.'

My uncle came toiling up the stairs, red in the face and short of breath. He had lingered on the floor below to talk to Mr Moffat. The Rifles officer wished him good day with a smile and went on downstairs.

'Who was that young fellow?' asked Uncle Nat.

'An officer of the 95th.'

'I could see that, but who is he?'

'A Captain Croft. He's brother to that tall, gaunt young man with a melancholy expression. They share a room on our floor.'

'Ah, I know who you mean. Ben will tell you about them, I'm sure. There's something I want to discuss with you. Carrie's gone up with her mother, so she'll still be with her. They were talking about hairstyles. I'll come in with you and show you what Moffat has lent me.'

We entered my room, which, as he supposed, was not occupied by Carrie, and he took a small bundle from his pocket. He unfolded the handkerchief on the table and revealed several pieces of jewellery: a diamond brooch and ring, a ruby pendant and a sapphire bracelet.

'Moffat wants me to value these,' he said. 'He says he received them from a client in payment of fees just before coming away.'

'I thought he'd been retired some time,' I said, 'but I suppose it could have been a long-standing debt.'

'Perhaps so. He says he has no idea of their value. I haven't had a chance to examine them yet, but I can tell they're costly.'

'Yes, I'm sure they are.'

'I don't want to trouble your aunt. You've always had your head screwed on, Elizabeth, and I'd be grateful for your opinion – in confidence, of course.'

'I'm not sure what to say. I'm no expert, unlike you, but I don't think I trust Mr Moffat.'

'Neither do I. There's something about him I don't entirely care for. I doubt if he could be relied on.'

'I thought there was something odd about that encounter in

the park with Lady Silbury. She seemed upset, but he was going to see her in her hotel. Do you think these jewels could belong to her?'

He shook his head. 'I don't know, but if she *has* given them to him it must be for a very good reason. Either she owes him money or—'

'Or he is extorting money from her under threat. What are you going to do?'

'What can I do? I'll value the items and given them back. Then I'll tell him I want nothing more to do with the matter. I've come here to get away from the business.'

He gathered up the jewels and put them back in his pocket.

'Don't say anything to your aunt or Carrie. They'll only make a fuss.'

'I know what you mean.'

'You're a good girl, Elizabeth. I sometimes think you're more of a daughter to me than Carrie.'

'Well, you have always been a good father.'

He patted my cheek and left the room. I was much intrigued by this latest development, but I thought my uncle's 'wait and see' attitude was probably the best.

My curiosity about the young Rifles officer and his mysterious brother was satisfied, as Uncle Nat suggested, by Ben. He seemed not to like Captain Croft.

'Oh, I've seen him about. He's staying here with his brother, the dark, miserable-looking chap you may have noticed. He's not in the army, but is some sort of impoverished landowner – Squire Lackland, looking for somewhere cheap to live, I suppose. Mama can cross him off the list for Carrie, at all events. He hasn't a bean – his father spent it all. That brother is even poorer – officers in the 95th aren't exactly rolling in riches.'

That was enough. I never mentioned the Croft brothers to him ever again.

By now I had sorted out all our fellow residents except one – and he remained an enigma for the time being, but was soon to loom large in all our lives. This was the former naval surgeon who had so rudely pushed past me at the door when I was talking to the sharp-featured man. I wondered who he was and why he was in Brussels. Although of no more than average height, he had a commanding presence and despite being not at all handsome his crisp, greying hair, piercing eyes and grim mouth caught my attention. He had a faint northern accent and spoke in a gruff, husky voice. I once overheard him talking to one of the chambermaids and was impressed by his excellent command of French. I discovered his name was Anthony Kean, but knew no more. Even Mr Moffat could supply no information.

The Moffats seemed to have appointed themselves our companions wherever we went, and I began to find them decidedly trying. One day, about a week after we had arrived in Brussels, we were all walking in the park and Mr Moffat was holding forth as usual on the latest developments.

'Bonaparte will stay within his own borders, you may be sure of that. We were led to believe that we would invade France on the 20th of next month.'

'Yes, Ben told us that,' agreed Aunt Hetty. 'It's common knowledge.'

'Ah, but I hear that the Duke has a ball planned for the 21st to celebrate the anniversary of Vittoria. The latest opinion is that we'll begin our campaign on the 25th.'

'Well, talk of the devil!' muttered Uncle Nat.

There, walking towards us, came a small group of men, mostly in uniform, but one, the most conspicuous by far, was in civilian dress: a well-made man of middle years and a little above medium height with striking Roman features. He was smiling and seemed perfectly at ease with his companions and his surroundings. To my amazement his head turned suddenly and his eyes were directed towards Carrie and me. He raised his hat and gave a small bow.

'He noticed us!' cried Aunt Hetty ecstatically when the group had gone by. 'He is so assured he inspires confidence – and so handsome! I didn't realise he had curly hair! Don't you think him handsome, girls?'

I agreed with her, feeling quite dizzy with excitement, but Carrie pulled a face.

'He's old. I detest old men.'

20

'He's forty-six, the same age as Bonaparte. That's middle-aged, not old,' I said.

'Quite!' said Aunt Hetty, rather annoyed as she had been born in the same year as the two opposing commanders.

'And I am sure', she added, 'that His Grace has all the energy and spirit of a young man.'

Carrie sighed. 'I suppose there's no shortage of women who think so.'

'Show some respect, Carrie!' said Aunt Hetty severely. 'He is our saviour, after all.'

'I find that remark blasphemous,' declared Mrs Moffat sententiously.

'Oh, I didn't mean it *that* way, I assure you. I was referring to the Duke as the saviour of Europe – in a military sense, that is.'

'Ah, but if you knew the truth! Joanna Southcott was to give birth to the true Saviour. He was to be known as Shiloh.'

'She was in her sixties and died of dropsy!' Mr Moffat cut in impatiently.

'So they said. Those of us who knew her suspected a plot by Certain Persons. It suited Certain Persons to remove her from the public domain. But when her box is opened all will be revealed and explained.'

'Really?' My aunt looked as though someone was telling her a fairy tale. 'How exciting! A magic box like Pandora's!'

'Not at all like Pandora's.'

'We came here to escape from that woman's pernicious influence,' said Mr Moffat irritably. 'Pray don't mention her again.'

'Very well,' said his wife sulkily, 'but the truth is the truth and it will out sooner or later.'

'Then let it be later!'

I glanced back along the path and saw a crowd of soldiers. Among the shakos was a black hat of a different shape, and among the scarlet coats one in drab. I recognised the usual garb of the sharp-featured man, who seemed to be minding everybody's business. Had he been watching us? I had the feeling we were going to see him again.

CHAPTER FOUR

The public ball at the Hôtel de Ville was, as Charles Croft predicted, a rather staid affair, despite its magnificent setting. Many of the participants were local burghers with a sprinkling of English visitors of the middling sort. Carrie dismissed them all as 'horrors', but there were plenty of officers to win her approval.

The ball began with a quadrille, for which I was obliged to accept Mr Moffat as a partner. I don't know why I was surprised to find him such a good dancer, but he was very sprightly and agile. As there were other people involved it was no great hardship to dance with him, but I hoped someone more amenable would appear.

The main difference from the assemblies I had attended in Birmingham was the prevalence of waltzing. At home this was still considered mildly scandalous. Even my aunt, who prided herself on keeping up with modern fashions, thought it 'rather fast', but here it was commonplace in every ballroom.

'I *suppose* it's all right,' she conceded, 'as there are some very respectable-looking people here, but it does look rather daring.'

'Let the girls enjoy themselves,' said my uncle indulgently. 'They are only young once.'

Carrie, looking very pretty in pale blue trimmed with rosebuds, revealed that she could waltz.

'When did you learn?' enquired Aunt Hetty, rather shocked.

'At school. One of the girls knew how and taught us all. Someone played the piano and we practised dancing with each other.'

'So much for education,' said my uncle with a smile.

'I'm sure Joanna Southcott did not approve of waltzing,' declared Mrs Moffat.

'I see no harm in it,' said her husband, eyeing the dancers with what looked like envy.

'Carrie, you may waltz with Benjie,' my aunt announced.

My cousins both looked aghast, but at last Ben said, 'Come along, sis, we'll have a twirl together and let Mama get used to the idea.'

That left me contemplating the enjoyment of others. I thought I looked pretty well that evening. Our maid Molly had excelled herself in dressing my hair and I wore a new dress of ivory crêpe with satin ribbons and the turquoise and pearl necklace I had inherited from my mother. Would I be condemned to Mr Moffat's closer company?

Suddenly there appeared at my side a vision of handsome masculinity: Charles Croft in full dress uniform.

Greetings were exchanged and he at once claimed the next dance. My aunt was quite overcome, but as he took me by the hand I hastily explained that I could not waltz.

'In that case I'll teach you. It won't take long; it's much easier than a quadrille or a cotillion. One-two-three! It couldn't be simpler. Let's go into the supper room – we can hear the music from there and it will be empty at this time apart from a few waiters and the like.'

The lesson which followed was extremely enjoyable.

'I feel as though I'm flying!' I gasped at last.

'That's because you're waltzing properly. I think we can take the floor now without fear of censure.'

We danced until we were dizzy and then sat out for a rest while Captain Croft bought ices.

'Isn't your brother here?' I asked.

'No, he doesn't dance. He says he can't afford to.'

'The chambermaid calls him "the English milord". He isn't really a lord, is he?'

'No, a mere baronet.'

'So he's *Sir* Henry Croft?'

'Yes, but he doesn't always use the title. It sometimes causes embarrassment in his present circumstances. People think you must have vast estates and lots of money. Henry has nothing: a decrepit ancient house that nobody wants to buy and a couple of hundred a year to live on. He lives in two or three rooms in one wing, looked after by Dobbs, that old chap you've seen about. He's butler, valet and housekeeper all in one. A charwoman comes in every day and a boy carries logs, does odd jobs and helps in the stable, though there's only one horse left. Henry wouldn't bring it with him, so we got our horses over here.'

'How did this happen? There must once have been an estate.'

'He had to sell everything to pay off the debts our father left. I'm afraid Croft senior was a rogue, though as his son I probably shouldn't say so. He was very charming, very devil-may-care. Everyone liked him, he was so easy, so pleasant and cheerful. Unfortunately he was a gambler, drank heavily and got into all sorts of scrapes. His liver gave out at last about five years ago. I was in the Peninsula at the time, so Henry had to cope on his own and did his best to settle our father's debts. It wasn't until I came home last year that I realised what a sorry state poor Henry was in. He made light of it in his letters, saying he didn't want to worry me when I was risking my life. He's been supplementing my pay, though he could ill afford to do so.

'An old aunt left him a small legacy which has enabled him to come here, and he's thinking of living abroad for a while as it's so much cheaper. I've told him he ought to find a rich widow to marry, but he was rather shocked. He's a little strait-laced, you know.'

'I think his conduct has been admirable. Not many men would beggar themselves from a sense of honour.'

'He had little choice. And now, I suppose I ought to return you to your family, though I must tell you I intend to dance with you again – and again, if you'll have me.'

'Of course, if you'll dance with my cousin Carrie.'

'The pretty little red-haired girl? That will hardly be an ordeal! But I beg you to dance with my friend Kincaid. He's very partial to brunettes, though one broke his heart in Spain.'

'Did she turn down his proposal?'

'He didn't get a chance to make one – a more enterprising fellow stepped in first. He still adores her from afar, but that doesn't stop him from waltzing with charming young ladies.'

'I'm flattered to be placed in that category.'

'Oh come, you must know you're the prettiest girl in the room.'

'That's an exaggeration. What about my cousin Carrie for a start?'

'She's very pretty, but she's fair. I've always thought fair girls insipid.'

On our return we found Ben had taken a Belgian girl as his partner and Carrie was circling the floor with a Black Brunswicker who could not speak a word of English, but bowed and clicked his heels in a very correct Germanic fashion.

'It was like dancing with an undertaker,' said Carrie when he had gone. 'Especially as he never spoke a word. Waltzing with a skull and crossbones is not very cheerful.'

'Then I will make up for it,' said Captain Croft. 'If you undertake to dance with me I'll talk all the time.'

He introduced me to Lieutenant Kincaid, who was hovering nearby. I had seen him once or twice before, but not made his acquaintance. He was a very tall, lanky, sunburnt young man with a humorous face, twinkling eyes and a delightful Scottish accent. I was more than happy to accept him as a dancing partner and reflected that this was much more enjoyable than our dull assemblies at home, where I was obliged to take the floor with earnest young doctors and lawyers or ambitious businessmen who could talk of nothing but making money.

When the time came for supper I went in with Charles Croft, following my aunt and uncle and the ubiquitous Moffats. Carrie brought up the rear on the arm of Lieutenant Kincaid, beside whom she looked like a little doll. Ben was nowhere to be seen and my aunt was peering about anxiously, convinced that some disaster had overtaken him.

'Who *are* these Moffats?' enquired Charles Croft. 'I've seen them in the hotel. Are they friends of yours?'

'Heavens, no! They came over on the same boat and seem to have attached themselves to us. He's a pleasant enough fellow – a retired lawyer and something of a busybody. He's rather tiresome in large doses. She is a recent devotee of Joanna Southcott and seems to put a damper on every occasion. There is something odd about them.'

I could not tell him about the jewels, though Mrs Moffat was wearing the diamond brooch on her purple satin gown.

'Do you know Lady Silbury?' I asked.

'Vaguely. I've seen her about. A rich widow, I think.'

'Mr Moffat was her lawyer before he retired. I saw them encounter each other and I got the impression she was afraid of him.

'Really?'

'I'm probably wrong.'

'No – we'll keep an eye on them.'

'Carrie calls them the Spratts. You know after Jack Spratt and his portly wife.'

Charles Croft let out a great, unselfconscious roar of laughter.

'What's the joke, Charlie? cried Lieutenant Kincaid from behind us.

'Ask your fair companion what she calls a certain odd couple who seem to be leading us in to supper.'

There was some laughter from Carrie and her escort.

We were soon seated round one of the tables consuming a cold collation. Charles Croft found himself between Mrs Moffat and me, and obviously decided to have some amusement at her expense as she began to tuck into a large plate of cold meats.

'Excuse me, ma'am, but is that pork on your plate?'

'Why, yes, I believe so: pork, beef and chicken.'

'Ah, I fear I can never face pork – not since an unfortunate incident in the Pyrenees. A couple of officers in the 28th actually ate the enemy for dinner. A Portuguese came round saying he had pork steaks for sale. My friends had a splendid meal, and it wasn't until afterwards that they realised they'd eaten portions of dead French soldiers.'

'Why are you telling me this, Captain Croft? It's enough to take away one's appetite.'

'Really, I'm so sorry: I wouldn't like it to do that. But I

heard your husband declare our army would eat the French for breakfast. I thought you might like to know it really happened. Shall I get one of the waiters to take your plate away? Perhaps you could have a simple salad or a few rusks or something?'

'No, I am quite satisfied with what I have here.'

She carefully placed the slices of pork on the side of her plate and cut into the beef.

'It ill behoves a young man about to face death to give such signs of frivolity,' she observed coldly.

'Eh?' said Captain Croft, as though he had never considered the idea. 'Oh, that won't do at all. I mean, one might feel a little apprehensive with a bullet in the heart, but it don't do to get all upset before it actually happens.'

At that moment my eye was caught by one of the waiters. I've no idea what made me look at him as one doesn't usually pay much attention to those who serve at table, but in this case I recognised the man. It was he who had come to my aid on the packet boat and had taken lodgings near the hotel. His gaze met mine and he smiled briefly, shook his head and placed his finger against his lips to indicate silence. I nodded, afterwards wondering why I had colluded with him to preserve his disguise. Why he had chosen to appear in this way I could not imagine. No doubt he had used bribery to gain entrance to the supper room, but to what purpose?

'There's Ben!' cried my aunt suddenly, waving to attract attention.

He was on the other side of the room, the candlelight shining on his red-gold head. If he saw his mother's signal he pretended not to notice. To my amazement his companions appeared to be Lady Silbury and her daughter.

'I'm surprised to see any of the nobility here tonight,' I said to my companion.

'Who? Where? Aha, a little odd to be sure, but of course there was a very grand reception here a few weeks ago attended by royalty. The building is certainly very splendid. Perhaps they thought tonight's ball would be equally aristocratic. Is that your cousin with them?'

'Yes, there's no mistaking his hair.'

'Did you know he was acquainted with them?'

'No, but I haven't any idea what he gets up to.'

My aunt wanted to go after Ben, but my uncle refused to move and insisted she should stay with him.

'Whatever he's doing and whoever he's with I'm sure he doesn't want us intruding. He's not exactly getting into bad company, is he?'

She bridled. 'Benjie is finding his own level, and I'm sure he'll tell us about it later.'

The second half of the evening passed in a delightful daze. As we drove back to the hotel in a cab I reflected that I had never enjoyed myself so much in all my life. I think I was a little in love with Charles Croft that night. It was not very deep or very serious, but it was all part of the happiness of the ball.

Carrie had also had a delightful time. She had not danced with the same man twice, nor with anyone in civilian dress.

I put to one side the strange occurrence during supper. If I ever encountered the sharp-featured man again I would ask him outright what his curious conduct signified. But until I fell asleep I would think of nothing but the intoxicating sensation of being whirled round the ballroom in the arms of a handsome young officer in Rifle green.

CHAPTER FIVE

The next few days after the ball passed very happily until Carrie and I were confronted with what we afterwards called 'the Horror in the Park'.

It really began one morning when I was again the first of our party to reach the open front door of our hotel. As on a previous occasion I saw the man in the drab coat leaning against a wall on the opposite side of the street. He raised his hat and bowed slightly, but did not attempt to come over to speak to me; instead he remained smoking his pipe.

Soon afterwards he was joined by a woman whom I saw approaching from the direction of the Place Royale. She was respectably but not elegantly dressed in a grey pelisse and a bonnet some years out of fashion. I thought she might be in her middle to late thirties.

I realised I had seen her in the park the previous day. She had been stopping people and talking to them. Some ignored her and brushed her aside, but she persevered and engaged in conversation with a number of others. At first I thought she was begging, but then it seemed to me that the shaking of heads indicated not an unwillingness to hand over money but an apologetic answer to her questions. She was trying to find out something, but not having any success.

Now she was talking to the strange man, who nodded and they both looked up at the windows of the hotel. A further discussion seemed to ensue and then he shook his head and pointed back along the street. After a few more words she turned and went back the way she came.

I was then joined by Carrie and my aunt and uncle. The encounter I had witnessed was banished from my mind until I recalled it all too vividly the following day.

The morning was hot and sultry, and as usual in such weather we made our way to the park. After enjoying a gentle stroll we sat on one of the benches in the shade of a tree.

'I wish we could see Captain Croft or Lieutenant Kincaid – preferably both,' whispered Carrie.

'So do I,' I agreed, beginning to feel rather bored, 'but at least we've been spared the company of the Moffats.'

Presently my aunt said she was thirsty and Uncle Nat said he was hungry.

'I need something to settle my stomach. They've no idea of a proper breakfast. The hot rolls were well enough, but as for cheese and radishes . . . ?' Words failed him.

'Carrie and I will go to the pavilion and bring you refreshments,' I volunteered.

'You will come straight back, won't you?' Aunt Hetty enquired anxiously. 'Don't get diverted or go off anywhere.'

'Where could we go?' said Carrie impatiently. 'We're not going to run off with a couple of officers. *I wish we could,*' she added in a whisper as we set off.

On our way through a wilder section of the park Carrie pointed out a little dingle to one side of the path.

'Couldn't we take a short cut through there?' she suggested. 'I'm sure it's nearer. Look, there's a track leading to below the bank.'

Before I could stop her she ran down the slope into the bushes.

'Oh!' she exclaimed. 'It's lovely here – so cool and shady. Oh!'

The second 'Oh!' was quite different from the first. She sounded startled and a little frightened.

I hastened down the path and found myself in a pretty dell, closely surrounded by greenery. The light seemed dim after the bright sunshine above.

Carrie pointed to a pair of feet: a woman's feet in much-mended half-boots, emerging from a bush. I parted the branches and found the body of a woman in a grey pelisse lying on her face. Her bonnet lay on top of her as though she had been dragged out of sight and her headgear flung after her. Her hair was loose and wildly disordered and what little I could see of her face was a curious blue. Oddly, I noticed her hands, the cheap gloves carefully darned.

'Is she dead?' whispered Carrie, backing away.

'Yes indeed, and it doesn't look natural.'

I felt cold and trembling and wondered what we should do next. We ought to get help immediately, of course, but when I seized Carrie by the arm and turned to go I found us face-to-face with the mysterious man in the drab coat.

'What have we here? Let me see.' He took a cursory look at the dead body, screening her from us as far as possible.

'This is very nasty. I'm sorry you young ladies had to find the poor creature.'

'She is *dead*, isn't she?' enquired Carrie anxiously, 'not unconscious from a fit or anything?'

'No, she's been dead some hours, I imagine. Strangled, by the look of it.'

'By a thief?' asked Carrie.

'I doubt if she had anything worth stealing. And as for the other obvious motive, I think not. Her clothes are undisturbed.'

'Now listen! You must leave everything to me. I'm sure you don't want to be questioned by the Belgian police, or perhaps involved in an inquest or court case. I'll say *I* found the body and you two ladies will not be mentioned. Now please say nothing to anyone or you may find yourself dragged into a very nasty business. I'll report this to the authorities and let them deal with it. Considering how many thousands of strangers are in the city they'll have their work cut out. Frankly, I doubt if they'll exert themselves very much. And in case you're wondering, I speak French pretty well after a year or two in a French gaol.'

'Gaol?' I was horrified.

'Prisoner of war – which makes it quite respectable.'

'But you know her!' I exclaimed. 'I saw you talking to her yesterday outside the hotel.'

'Indeed, I saw you in the doorway. She was asking for directions and I suggested she should go back to the park. She was looking for her husband and wondered if he was in the hotel. I'll explain all this to anyone making enquiries.'

'You think she was a soldier's wife trying to find her husband?'

'Probably. Whether she found him and he wasn't altogether pleased to see her is a possible explanation of the tragedy. But you must go now and try to carry on normally. Put this business out of your heads. You can trust me.'

'But we don't even know your name,' I protested.

'Fox. Jeremiah Fox – Jerry for short,' he said with a grin. 'Don't look so worried. Calm yourselves and go back to the main path.'

'Were you following us?' Carrie asked the question over her shoulder as we moved away.

'Ah,' he smiled. 'That would be telling!'

We were both badly shaken and alarmed, but neither of us wished to be involved. I realised that what I should have done was run out into the main pathways of the park and found a mature British officer to tell of our discovery. He would have known what to do. Fox's sudden appearance at the scene had driven such thoughts out of my head. I was a fool to have trusted Fox, but I was longing to get away.

We continued with our original plan, having agreed to say nothing to Uncle Nat and Aunt Hetty. When we reached the pavilion we found ourselves surrounded by cheerful people: laughing soldiers, children with toys, customers buying rolls to feed the ducks on the lake. Everything seemed so normal and pleasant that our gruesome discovery appeared no more real than the recollection of a bad dream. We bought lemonade and sandwiches and returned by a different route.

'You've been a long time,' said my aunt. 'What delayed you?'

'We tried to take a short cut and got lost and then we had to wait a while to be served,' said Carrie, with all the aplomb of a born liar.

A couple of days later I caught sight of the man in the drab coat in the street outside our hotel and ran after him.

'Mr Fox!' I cried. 'I must have a word with you. I've been so troubled by that dreadful discovery we made. Can you tell me any more?'

'Not a great deal,' he said cautiously. "Once I'd let the Belgian authorities take over and they'd cleared me of any suspicion they were reluctant for me to know any more. The woman was English, as we supposed, but what her name was, who she was looking for and whether she found him or not I still do not know. I imagine she was the wife of a soldier who had abandoned her. No doubt enquiries will be made with the military authorities.'

I wondered if he was telling me all he knew; I felt he was keeping something back, but he seemed eager to move away.

'Try to forget the whole matter, my dear young lady. There's enough tragedy in the world – and more to come very soon, I've no doubt. A nation on the verge of war is not likely to expend much energy investigating the death of an obscure stranger.'

He laid his finger against his lips as I had seen him do at the Hôtel de Ville in his disguise as a waiter.

'Discretion is the word, Miss Aston. Keep quiet about this unhappy event or you may find yourself in danger.' He walked away.

Danger? What on earth did he mean?

I worried for some time over this – unlike Carrie, who seemed to have put it out of her mind. Then other events intervened and 'the Horror in the Park' receded until it seemed like a play once seen in the theatre and of as little consequence.

CHAPTER SIX

Towards the end of May a grand cavalry review was held at Ninove, about fifteen miles from Brussels. Everyone seemed to be going, so Uncle Nat hired a comfortable old barouche to convey us to the site of the spectacle. The coachman spoke few words of English, so I was called on to translate any orders my uncle gave him. Ben said he would accompany us on horseback.

The day was brilliantly bright and sunny and promised great warmth. The roads were full of carriages, some adorned with the crests or coats of arms of noble families, all heading west. We saw the Moffats in a hired gig.

'It's a wonder it doesn't tip over on Mrs Spratt's side,' observed Carrie maliciously.

The journey itself was interesting. Uncle Nat pointed out the rich, fertile appearance of the countryside and the extraordinary height of the crops, but Aunt Hetty and Carrie were more taken by the children who ran alongside the carriage, turning somersaults and calling out in their shrill voices:

'Vive le Roi d'Angleterre! Vive Vellington!'

Uncle Nat threw them coins which increased their enthusiasm.

'Vive les Anglais!' they shouted.

We broke the journey halfway to take refreshment at an inn and rest the horses. Ben was nowhere to be seen, which caused my aunt some consternation.

'Oh, stop fretting about him, Hetty,' said my uncle, showing unusual impatience. 'He's old enough to look after himself and he's a soldier, for heaven's sake! What harm can he have come to when the road's full of English people? And here are two from our hotel now.'

I looked up, expecting to behold the Moffats, and was delighted to see the two Croft brothers approaching us and asking if they might share our table. Charles introduced his brother, whom we had seen about the hotel and occasionally at the theatre or in the park, but we were not until now on speaking terms. Once or twice he had stood aside for me in one of the window embrasures on the stairs and had bowed and given a faint smile.

My first impression had been of a rather withdrawn, melancholy young man. I had thought him older than thirty until Charles told me his age. Perhaps his anxieties had aged him. Already there were a few silver threads in his dark hair and faint lines between his brows and running from his nose to the corners of his mouth. One could see what he would become in middle age. He was certainly less handsome than his brother, but I found something attractive in his thin, aquiline face and serious expression.

As I found him sitting beside me I began to engage him in conversation; and after a commonplace exchange on the subject of the weather, the state of the roads and the congestion of the traffic, I decided to try a bolder approach in order to break his reserve.

'Sir Henry,' I said, 'your brother tells me you rarely use your title. Are you using it today or are you being very modest and humble?'

To my delight he laughed. 'I can't afford to be anything else. Charles says whatever comes into his head and is considered amusing. I have no small talk and am thought to be dull.'

'I am sure that is not so.'

'Charles has had all the adventures and is likely to have more in the near future. My life has been comparatively uneventful: rotten parchment bonds rather than battlefields.'

'But you have done what is honourable and have sacrificed your own comfort and pleasure to do so. That is just as admirable as your brother's gallantry.'

'I am glad you think so; not many would. I see Charles has explained the situation to you. Perhaps you know that I'm thinking of living over here for a while as it's so much cheaper. However, the forthcoming campaign may change everything. The Duke seems very easy-going and sanguine about the whole affair, but I wonder how much of his cheerful manner is assumed in order to prevent a panic in Brussels? From what I've heard, he's very different among those closest to him.'

At that moment a figure I recognised entered the room: a sharp-featured man in a drab coat. He glanced round him and then observed us at the corner table.

He came over, bowed slightly, then murmured, 'A word in your ear, sir,' and bent to whisper something to my uncle, who changed countenance.

Before Uncle Nat could say anything the man withdrew. Other people made way for him and he was out of the door in an instant.

'What a rude man!' exclaimed my aunt, but Uncle Nat shook his head.

'I don't know what to make of him. He just told me that Ben has gone off, which we knew. Then he said he was in pursuit of Lady Silbury's daughter and he thought we ought to know.'

Aunt Hetty looked mollified. 'Ah well, he wishes to join people of his own sort,' she said.

'Who was that man?' enquired Henry Croft curiously. 'I've seen him about, but I can't make him out at all.'

'His name is Fox,' I said, 'but I know nothing more about him save that he is in lodgings down the road from our hotel. He seems to find out everyone's business. I'm not surprised by what he told us about my cousin Ben. He is a complete snob. I'm sure he's ashamed of his own family, especially his father.'

No one could have taken Uncle Nat for a gentleman, though he dressed well and had natural good manners. His Brummagen accent and plebeian features would always give him away.

'I see no reason why he should be,' observed Sir Henry. 'What is his occupation?'

'A jeweller in Birmingham.'

'Ah, I thought I knew the accent. But you don't have it.'

'No, I was sent to a genteel school for young ladies in Bath. My cousin Carrie was sent there later, but hated it and was brought home and sent to a local day school.'

Some boisterous young officers in Rifle green entered at that moment, hailing Charles Croft with shouts of delight.

He excused himself from our table and joined them with much laughter and cries of 'For God's sake don't drink their beer – it tastes of cow dung! Wine all round – Rhenish is cheap enough unless anyone fancies Hollands!'

'I fear I've lost him for the day.' Henry Croft smiled ruefully. 'It's understandable. They share his life more than I do. I'll ride beside your barouche, if that doesn't displease you.'

'Quite the opposite,' I said, and then wondered if I was too bold, but he smiled and looked more cheerful than for some time.

The Moffats entered just then and Aunt Hetty waved to them, but as the room was very crowded, and every seat taken, they withdrew looking very disgruntled.

'Are they friends of yours?' enquired Sir Henry.

'Acquaintances merely. I can't say I like them very much. Mrs Moffat casts gloom in every direction and Mr Moffat is a little *too* friendly.'

'I know what you mean. He tried once to impose his fellowship on me by asking a great many questions, some of them quite impertinent. I must admit I gave him the cold shoulder. Not that I care!'

'I must say I am very glad that you and your brother managed to join us before the Moffats arrived. The food is indifferent, but the company superior.'

He smiled again and I felt an unspoken exchange of sympathy. This was not like being whirled round in a waltz by the dashing Charles, but it was warmer, deeper and made me long for a continuing friendship. There was no more than that at present, but he was the only man I had ever met who had aroused such feelings.

The traffic became quite heavy as more and more vehicles converged on the road to Ninove. At last we reached the level meadows in the bend of the River Dender where the cavalry had already assembled. I was much taken with the curious contrast between the placid countryside and the busy, warlike scene in its midst.

With the help of the Croft brothers – for Charles had joined us when we arrived at the site of the review – we were able to secure a good place from which to observe the spectacle.

The flat, rich fields stretched to a wooded ridge, the tall grass waving in a gentle breeze. A temporary bridge had been erected over the river for the Duke of Wellington's entourage to pass across. Everywhere an orderly bustle was in progress; every soldier was in his shirtsleeves, rubbing down horses, burnishing accoutrements, polishing everything in sight.

'There must be thousands of them!' exclaimed my uncle.

'Six thousand!' declared Charles. 'It's confounded hot. I don't envy those fellows having to stand to attention for His Lordship. Everyone hates reviews, especially in this sort of weather. I've brought my field glass. I thought you might like to borrow it to get a better view of the proceedings.' He handed it to my aunt with an engaging smile.

'How thoughtful! Thank you so much, Captain Croft. I'll pass it on to the others in turn.'

Charles stayed a little longer and then rode off among the crowd of spectators, picking out numerous friends and acquaintances. He returned just as the cavalry and artillery were drawn up for inspection. The hussars were in front, in open formation so that a scarlet wall of heavy dragoons could be seen behind them, the sun glittering on their plumed helmets. Beyond these were ranged light dragoons in blue uniforms and battalions of horse artillery flanked the whole.

'So beautiful!' I murmured. 'And I know it's silly, but it makes me sad.'

'I know exactly what you mean,' said Sir Henry softly.

'It's a fine sight, to be sure!' exclaimed Charles Croft, 'though I must admit to a slight prejudice in favour of light infantry. However, here come Their Lordships and Prince-ships and Almighty-ships!'

A great cheer went up and the artillery fired a salute as the Duke's cortège approached. His retinue displayed a fantastic variety of uniforms and every European decoration as it clattered across the bridge.

Aunt Hetty stood up eagerly, Charles's telescope pressed to her eye.

'Oh, there's the Duke! He looks even finer in uniform and on a horse. So handsome and soldierly! One feels safe just looking at him.'

'*You* may, madam, but I swear the French don't,' grinned Charles.

'I believe she's smitten!' observed Uncle Nat amiably. 'I wonder if I can persuade him to run off with her.'

'I'm afraid Mrs Wakefield would have to take her turn,' Charles told him. 'Our commander-in-chief is very popular with the ladies. At present a certain blonde beauty holds sway.'

'Really?' My aunt did not know whether she ought to appear shocked or intrigued.

'Who is that old fellow with a big white moustache like a walrus?' she continued, changing the subject.

'Prince Blücher, of course. The pleasant-looking man with the round rosy face is Lord Hill – Daddy Hill, because he cares for his men like a father. And the very handsome, tall man in hussar uniform is Lord Uxbridge, who commands all the cavalry.'

At first it was interesting to hear Charles pointing out all the notables, but as soon as the actual inspection began, boredom set in. My uncle fell asleep, overcome by the heat, and Carrie and I descended from the barouche to stretch our legs. Charles carried off my cousin to introduce her to his friends and it seemed to be tacitly understood that I would be left to accompany Sir Henry.

'You must not take too much notice of my brother,' he said as we strolled together along the line of carriages. 'He is an impudent scoundrel.'

'He is a very charming young man, and his manner is not at all unbecoming in a soldier. But you are not at all alike. Perhaps it is due to the difference in age.'

'Only four years. We were brought up by servants in our infancy. Our mother died when Charles was born and we hardly ever saw our father. We were both sent away to a rather indifferent school and Charles joined the army at sixteen. I was sent to Oxford, but had to leave after a year because the fees weren't paid.' He smiled ruefully. 'So you see what a disordered, ramshackle upbringing I've had.'

I noticed that a number of rather grand people in crested carriages acknowledged my companion as we went by. One or two of the men even called out to him, and several ladies smiled and waved their fans. He returned their greetings with a solemn expression and a stiff bow.

'You seem to know a great many people of rank,' I observed.

'*They* know *me*, more like! I've never mixed in that sort of society; I can't afford it, for one thing, but there's a smaller set here in Brussels. They're eager to rope in anyone they consider to be well bred. I can't think why. I'm not good company and I'm hardly the sort who'd be considered an eligible catch for a daughter. But my father was well liked for all his failings – perhaps because of them. He had a great deal of charm, like Charles.'

'Charm is a very superficial attribute. Charles has a great deal more to him than that.'

'Of course he has, but my poor father had little else except a capacity for ruining his descendants.'

I noticed, not for the first time, that his boots were well polished but decidedly old and had, I fancied, been repaired many times.

He steered me between two curricles to the rear of the carriages.

'We'll be less observed here,' he said. 'Everyone is facing the other way.'

We were not, however, free from curious eyes as there were many people behind the spectators: coachmen drinking beer, footmen flirting with maids, and, a few yards further along the path, two figures I instantly recognised, enjoying a companionable smoke together as they lounged on the grass, one with a pipe and the other with a cigar. It was 'Jack Tar', as Carrie called him, and the mysterious Mr Fox.

'I think we know those two, by sight at least. I didn't realise they were acquainted,' remarked Sir Henry.

The two men acknowledged us with a wave of the pipe and a

smile from Drab Coat and a scowling nod from his companion.

'I feel that something is going on of which we know nothing,' I said. 'Possibly Mr Moffat is mixed up in it too.'

'You could be right, but there are more important matters brewing which could throw all other plans and conspiracies out of the window. Now, I've told you a little of my early life. Perhaps you could tell me something of yours. I take it you have no parents as you are travelling with an uncle and aunt.'

I explained that I had lost both parents when I was six; but despite that tragedy, my childhood had been happier than his and certainly more secure.

I had wondered, briefly, whether to confide in Sir Henry about the incident in the park, which now seemed curiously remote and unreal. However, the conversation had taken a more personal turn and the opportunity had passed.

We returned at last to the hired barouche, where my aunt and uncle – now roused from his sleep – were preparing to alight.

'I really must stretch my legs a little,' said Aunt Hetty. 'It will be a long drive home and I've been sitting down a great deal.'

'I'll get out first and give you a hand,' said Uncle Nat.

He descended rather clumsily. The steps were already lowered, but there was no sign of the coachman.

Aunt Hetty still held her parasol, rather foolishly as it transpired, as it meant she had only one hand to extend to my uncle. None of us, not even my aunt, was quite sure how it happened. I think she was possibly distracted by a trumpet call as her head turned slightly, but she missed the steps completely, let go of my uncle's outstretched hand, and fell awkwardly on the ground.

Uncle Nat bent to assist her, but she shrieked, 'Don't touch me. I can't get up. I think I've broken my leg.'

CHAPTER SEVEN

An accident always attracts a crowd. In a few seconds my aunt was surrounded by a host of spectators, all trying to help and offer advice. Charles and Carrie were on the way back and hastened to join us.

'I have some knowledge of injuries,' said Charles. 'If I may—'

'I have even more knowledge – I'm a surgeon!' said a deep, authoritative voice and the thickset man with greying hair shouldered his way through the crowd and knelt beside my aunt. She was obviously very frightened and protested when he drew back the hem of her skirt.

'I can't possibly assess the damage until I've had a look,' he declared. 'Now, this may hurt. Has anyone any brandy?'

Inevitably a flask was produced and I found her smelling salts in her reticule. Aunt Hetty did her best to be brave.

'A simple fracture of the tibia,' the surgeon announced. 'I'll need splints and bandages.'

Charles at once offered to run for one of the army surgeons who were stationed in tents behind the cavalry lines. Meanwhile, my aunt was made more comfortable with cushions from the coach, and Carrie and I sat beside her on the grass and tried to distract her.

'What will become of me?' she moaned. 'How will I ever get back to the hotel?'

'In the carriage, of course,' said the surgeon. 'We'll put a plank across the seats – suitably padded, of course – and you can stretch your legs across it. I'm afraid it won't be altogether comfortable, but at least you'll get home without doing any further damage.'

My uncle, who was pale with anxiety and shock, asked our new friend his name.

'Kean, like the actor. Anthony Kean, late of His Majesty's Ship *Callisto*. I was their surgeon.'

'Ah, then you must be used to dealing with broken bones.'

'I should hope so. I've seen far worse than this. But she'll have to rest the leg for at least six weeks to give the bones a chance to knit.'

'How shall we get her upstairs? There are a hundred steps up to our room. We're on the third floor.'

'We'll worry about that when we get there.'

I was aware of another problem. If my aunt was to occupy two seats in a four-seater carriage, then one of us would have no comfortable way of returning to Brussels. I resigned myself to travelling on the box with the driver, but fate decreed otherwise.

Charles returned with an army surgeon who looked hot and harassed.

'We've had many faintings and falls this afternoon with this hot weather. You're lucky we have splints to spare,' he said.

He and Kean exchanged a few words on the condition of the patient, and the newcomer, on examining my aunt's leg, agreed on the diagnosis.

'I'll set it,' said Mr Kean, 'so she can travel safely.'

However, as soon as he seized the damaged limb my aunt screamed and fainted.

'Don't revive her,' he instructed. 'With any luck I can do this before she comes round. She won't be very comfortable, but she'll be spared the worst of the pain.'

He worked swiftly and Aunt Hetty was securely strapped up in whalebone splints before she regained consciousness. Sir Henry, who had disappeared when his brother returned, came back with a board, which was padded with cushions and placed across the seats of the carriage. Charles jumped up inside, Mr Kean, carefully gathering the patient up in his arms, handed her up to him and he settled her into her seat.

The army surgeon produced a dose of laudanum, which presently made her rather sleepy.

'I think you'd better go back to Brussels immediately,' he said. 'The review will continue for some time and you need to escape the traffic when everyone starts the homeward journey.'

My uncle sat beside Aunt Hetty, and Carrie occupied the seat opposite.

'Oh dear,' she said, 'what is poor Lizzie to do?'

'Perhaps the box,' suggested Uncle Nat, 'though it's not very comfortable or safe.'

'I came on a borrowed horse,' said Mr Kean. 'One of the officers in the hotel had a spare and was kind enough to lend it to me.'

'I have an idea! ' cried an all-too-familiar voice.

I might have known Mr Moffat would appear, though fortunately he was too late to help.

'We came in a hired gig,' he said. 'I presume you can drive a gig, Mr Kean?'

'Oh yes, my father was a farmer. But—'

'Just wait one moment. I'm sure Lady Silbury will be able to convey my wife and me back to Brussels in her carriage. It seats four and only she and her daughter occupy it.'

Off he scampered, leaving the rest of us somewhat nonplussed.

'I'll tell you one thing,' Charles Croft murmured in my ear. 'On my way to fetch the surgeon I saw that cousin of yours, Ben Wakefield, sitting in the Silbury barouche with Her Ladyship and that daughter of hers. He'd taken his cap off for some reason and that hair of his shone like a beacon.'

'They were together at the ball at the Hôtel de Ville,' I reminded him. 'I don't know what's going on. He wouldn't confide in me.'

'On my way back he was still there and I called to him to get back to his mother as she'd been hurt. I haven't seen him since.'

At that moment, Ben appeared, looking decidedly sheepish, and had to be informed of the events of the last half-hour. He hastened to run round the carriage to comfort his mama.

'Benjie, how good of you to come,' she murmured sleepily. 'How kind and unselfish to console your silly old mother when you could be enjoying yourself.' She yawned and closed her eyes.

Mr Moffat came back to announce that Lady Silbury was only too delighted to offer transport to his wife and him, and consequently the gig was free for Mr Kean and Miss Aston. He trotted off with an expression of smug satisfaction.

'Come along, then,' said the naval surgeon. 'I'm going to drive directly behind the barouche so I can keep an eye on my patient. You'll be more comfortable in the gig than on the box and I hope my conversation may be more interesting than that of a Belgian coachman, though I believe you speak good French.'

'Moderately good,' I admitted, 'though I've an idea any exchange with the coachman would be rather stilted. What about your horse?'

'I'm sure he'll trot behind us if we fix up a lead.'

I had an idea that Mr Kean was not going to be easy to engage in conversation, and I was right. Perhaps the coachman would have been easier after all. We began the journey in silence and then I decided to make an effort.

'It is very kind of you to take care of my aunt,' I ventured.

'It's nothing. It's my job,' he said abruptly.

I made some commonplace remarks such as I had used with Sir Henry Croft, but whereas this had led to an easy exchange, this time I received nothing but grunts and monosyllables. I would have to either try another tack or sit in silence for fifteen miles.

'Don't you find it strange how Mr Moffat imposes on Lady Silbury? She is so far above him in society, I can't see why she should let the Moffats ride in her carriage.'

'Wasn't he a lawyer or something?'

'Yes, but I get the impression she's a little afraid of him.'

'Ah well, lawyers sometimes know too much.'

'I suppose so, but he seems a little too sure of himself. I'm sure he's responsible for introducing my cousin Ben to Lady Silbury's daughter. Does she know my uncle's in trade?'

'What sort of trade?'

'He's a jeweller. We have no pretensions to gentility.'

'Sounds good enough to me, but then, I've never pretended to be anything I'm not.'

'I think I detect the North in your voice.'

'Yes, I was born in Yorkshire. I've never quite lost the accent even after twenty years at sea.'

'I suppose you've been put on half-pay like so many naval officers.'

'No,' he said shortly, giving me a calculating look as though determining whether I was to be trusted. 'I might as well tell you,' he continued, 'I'm *not* on half-pay. I only wish I was. I have a little prize money, and at present I'm living on that. I'm hoping to find work as a surgeon over here. When the big battle comes I'll be needed. Then I might find more regular employment.'

'But why aren't you given your due? Surely after all those years at sea . . . I'm sorry, I've no right to ask.'

'You've as much right as anyone else. That Moffat fellow found out. So did another chap. Something went wrong. I had to operate on the Captain – an amputation of his arm. It went amiss and he died.'

'That sort of consequence is not altogether unusual, is it?'

'Try telling that to the Admiralty! If it had been an ordinary seaman no one would have cared except his mates, but it was the Captain, who had friends in high places. Someone had to take the blame.'

'It's so unfair!'

'So is life!'

His tone was so bitter I did not pursue the subject and we lapsed into silence. Clouds of dust arose from the road and I lowered the veil of my bonnet to keep it from my face. Perhaps I also felt it acted as some sort of screen between me and my companion, who seemed lost in some angry reverie, scowling and snarling at the horse.

We stopped at the inn where we had taken refreshment on the way down. Lemonade and sandwiches were brought out to us. Mr Kean got down to talk to my aunt and to make sure she was resting her leg and not enduring too great a discomfort. She managed to drink, but refused food.

Suddenly an elegant barouche with a crest on the door went whirling by. I caught a glimpse of Lady Silbury's face, set rigidly in an expression of disapproval. Mr Moffat waved to us gaily as they were swept away in a cloud of dust.

Three horsemen caught up with us and dismounted: the Croft brothers and my cousin Ben, who went immediately to his mother.

'How are you getting on with the jolly Jack Tar?' murmured Charles in my ear.

'Jolly he certainly is not. He seems rather a grim and bitter man – with every cause, from what he told me. I wish you were driving the gig; you'd keep me amused. I feel the need for someone to cheer me at present.'

'Never mind, only another seven miles or so. He seems a pretty good surgeon at all events. That dragoon sawbones was quite impressed. I'm sure your aunt is in good hands.'

'Something about that man troubles me,' said Sir Henry quietly. 'I don't quite know what it is. Perhaps it's just his manner.'

'I must go,' I excused myself. 'At least I'm between my family and my friends. I'll try to find out more.'

Mr Kean rejoined the gig munching a ham roll. Like my aunt I was thirsty but not hungry and had accepted only a glass of lemonade.

When we resumed our journey I asked Mr Kean about the sharp-featured man in the drab coat.

'I find Mr Fox rather mysterious,' I said. 'I saw you enjoying a smoke with him and I thought he might be a friend.'

'I scarcely know him. He's in lodgings near the hotel. We've exchanged a few words once or twice, and when he offered me a cigar today it seemed churlish to refuse. I don't know who or what he is, but he seems privy to everybody's business.'

'That's what I thought. So does Mr Moffat, but in a different way. He's a toad-eater, but I don't think Fox is.'

'No. He seems to know a lot about the army and I asked if he'd ever been a soldier and he admitted he had. More than that he wouldn't say.'

For the rest of the journey we talked of the forthcoming campaign, of Bonaparte and Wellington and the strangely festive and unwarlike atmosphere of Brussels. We arrived at the hotel to find the Moffats awaiting us with Madame Dubois.

'All is arranged!' he cried. 'Everything is settled. There is not a spare room to be had, but my good wife and I occupy a spacious chamber on the first floor and the easiest solution, my dear Mr Wakefield, is for you to take it and we will go up to the third floor and occupy your accommodation. This will avoid having to carry poor Mrs Wakefield up a hundred steps, which would be very difficult and could cause further injury.'

'All our clothes and possessions must be exchanged, so Madame Dubois has made arrangements, dear Mrs Wakefield, for you to rest on her sofa in her private parlour until everything is in order.'

My aunt and uncle were naturally grateful, but I fancied Mrs Moffat was not at all pleased. No doubt she did not relish heaving her bulk up a hundred steps every day.

I was not too delighted myself. Although I was glad Aunt Hetty would be comfortably settled, I did not like the idea of being stranded on the third floor with the Moffats next door.

'Benjie will be just down the passage,' said my aunt consolingly, 'and I'm sure that's a comfort.'

I was not at all sure about that. I was much more cheered by the thought that the Croft brothers would also be near at hand.

CHAPTER EIGHT

In the second week of June a picnic was arranged by the Croft brothers in the Forêt de Soignes. There were fifteen of us in the party and the day promised to be fair, despite the threat of thunderstorms.

At first we thought we would not be able to go as Aunt Hetty demanded constant attention. However, my uncle declared that he would stay behind and look after her so that Carrie and I could go on the expedition.

'But chaperones!' she cried. 'All those young men! I know our Benjie will be there, but it will still look bad.'

'The Moffats are going,' said Uncle Nat, 'and I'm sure Mrs Moffat is a very monument to morality. She can chaperone the girls. They've earned a little pleasure this last week after being at your beck and call. Let them enjoy themselves. I did hear that several other ladies will be present.'

'Who?' demanded my aunt suspiciously.

'I don't know, but some very respectable ladies, I'm assured.'

'I don't think Sir Henry Croft would sanction the presence of anyone who *wasn't* respectable,' I said.

'Well, yes,' she conceded, 'he seems a very sober and upright young man, though I'm not sure that description also applies to his brother. He seems given to levity and I think he's inclined to flirt.'

'That's his way,' I told her. 'I believe seasoned soldiers like Charles Croft put on a rather frivolous manner to make light of the horrors of war.'

Our party set out in great high spirits through the Namur Gate.

All the men were on horseback, but Carrie and I were obliged to share the Moffats' hired barouche. I soon realised that another carriage was following us at a distance and I could glimpse plumed bonnets bobbing inside, but I was not near enough to see who it was.

Charles Croft and his brother had gone out a few days before to find a suitable spot for us to settle, so the two of them were leading the way on their sturdy Flemish horses.

The forest consisted almost entirely of beech trees which were in nearly full foliage and provided welcome shade from the glare of the sun. Mr Moffat chattered away merrily without ceasing. I did not listen.

We came at last to a delightful glade, not too far from the road, where we halted. Rugs were spread out, baskets and hampers unloaded, cushions distributed to the ladies, and all was as cheerful and comfortable as could be.

I soon discovered that the other carriage contained Lady Silbury, her daughter and a companion. They sat a little apart from the rest of us with Ben dancing attendance. I then recollected a fragment of Mr Moffat's monologue, which I had only noticed on account of the name.

'Lady Silbury is honouring us with her presence, along with her daughter, the Honourable Lydia, and Miss Barlow, the companion. The latter is some sort of poor relation who has acted as governess for the family.'

I wondered how Her Ladyship had been persuaded to join a party so much her inferior in rank. Once again I suspected Mr Moffat's coercion. Ben insisted on presenting Carrie and me to her after hissing a warning not to say anything about our family.

Lady Silbury was graciously condescending, which I found irritating. I suspected she was rather stupid and felt sorry for her daughter, a meek, pleasant-looking girl of about Carrie's age.

'Lieutenant Wakefield has told me a little about you. I believe your mother had an unfortunate accident at the cavalry review. I trust she is making a good recovery?'

'Very good, thank you, ma'am,' said Carrie demurely. 'My papa is staying with her so we could come to the picnic.'

'Your father owns land in Warwickshire, I understand,' she continued.

Ben looked decidedly uncomfortable and glared at his sister. I wondered what he had told Lady Silbury about his background. He must have given the impression that the house on Summer Hill (admittedly in Warwickshire) was some sort of manor with an estate.

Carrie obviously did not know what to say, so I intervened. 'I am sure Ben has told you everything about our circumstances,' I said.

'And you, Miss Aston, are the cousin who was brought up by your uncle and aunt. Quite a credit to them, I should say.' She eyed me approvingly.

I suppose I should have felt gratified, but I really did not care what she thought. I stared at Ben, who shuffled awkwardly.

'We really must return to our friends, who have provided refreshments for us. Thank you so much for receiving us.'

I was about to move away but Her Ladyship had not finished.

'Your friends? Ah, the Croft brothers. A very good old family! Such a tragedy, what happened! Their father was a gamester, you know, and drank heavily.' She sighed deeply. 'Everyone thinks Sir Henry is very noble, but quite foolish to do what he has done – beggared himself to pay off the debts. He rarely goes into society now. I don't know what will become of him. Would you ask him to come over here and have a few words with me? I trust you are being properly chaperoned as your mother is not here.'

'Mrs Moffat is doing that service, ma'am.'

'Ah, a strange woman! A devotee of the late Joanna Southcott. One need say no more. But she *is* perfectly respectable, I'm sure.'

I bobbed a curtsey and led Carrie away.

'What's Ben up to?' she whispered. 'I think he's trying to give the impression that Papa is some sort of country squire. He's trying to woo that Lydia girl. I longed to tell Her Ladyship that Ben's father is a jeweller from Birmingham.'

'We'll keep that in reserve. Let Ben fret a little. I like to see him disconcerted.'

When we returned to the spot Charles had chosen for us his

brother indicated that I should sit next to him. I was pleased to agree, but told him that Lady Silbury wished to speak to him.

'I can't think why,' he groaned, scrambling to his feet.

'She says you are a good old family.'

'So we are, I suppose, which is more than can be said for the late Lord Silbury or for Her Ladyship. Her father was a nobody who made his fortune in the West Indies. People of that sort are always snobs.'

While he was absent the refreshments were shared out: cold chicken and ham, salad, cheesecakes, custards, strawberries and apricots. Charles Croft and his friend Johnny Kincaid dispensed champagne.

'Only four shillings, a bottle – we must make the most of it!' he cried. 'Lemonade for those who don't imbibe,' he added, proffering some to Mrs Moffat, who viewed it with suspicion.

'Are you quite sure it's not in any respect alcoholic?'

'Not in the slightest,' he assured her, 'and I can guarantee you will not be assaulted by the rude and drunken soldiery in our party.'

Sir Henry threw himself down beside me.

'Thank goodness that's over! What a tiresome woman! She thinks you are quite a refined young lady, so you obviously made a good impression on her.'

'I really don't care.'

He chuckled. 'I didn't think you would. Here, have some chicken.'

'We have *two* tiresome women in the party,' said Charles, rejoining us. 'When I look at them I wonder what we are fighting for; but when I look at you two girls *I know*.'

'A charming compliment!' said Carrie, flirtatiously. Finding herself between Charles and Kincaid she was in seventh heaven.

Most of the party were from our hotel, but there were a couple of officers I did not recognise. Mr Kean was not present and I remarked on his absence to my companion.

'He was invited – I think we owed him that after what he's done for your aunt, but he said he'd rather not come as he was no use in society. I said neither was I, but he shrugged and said

52

it was different for him. I let it go at that.'

After a while, Lady Silbury retired to sit in her carriage with a novel, leaving Lydia in the care of Miss Barlow.

'Lady Silbury's daughter seems a nice girl,' said Sir Henry, 'but completely under her mother's thumb. Your cousin will have a problem there.'

'More than one, I think; he has not been entirely honest with them. He has led them to believe his situation is much superior to what it is in reality.'

'Then what does he intend? Is he going to run off with her before her mother discovers the truth?'

'I wouldn't put anything past him. He is not to be trusted.'

Mrs Moffat, overcome by the heat and the food, dozed off beneath her parasol, but her husband, fully alert, was eager to join in the games of the young officers. These had grown boisterous, whether from the influence of the champagne or from youthful high spirits I could not tell. They were soon romping about like great overgrown schoolboys.

Blind man's bluff was suggested, followed by catch as catch can and then progressing to various chasing games of their own invention.

I found myself hauled to my feet by Charles Croft.

'Come on, you must join in. I know it's silly, but it's great fun.'

So it was. I saw Ben snatch the Honourable Lydia away from the protesting governess/companion and run off with her among the trees. We scampered about in all directions, giggling helplessly and eventually growing out of breath. At one point I encountered Carrie, who was looking flushed and dishevelled.

'That horrid Moffat tried to kiss me,' she complained. 'Who *does* he think he is? Why should he want to join in a game with young people?'

'I'd have said that was obvious.'

'I let young Parker kiss me – he's so sweet, but far too young for me.'

'He's near your age.'

'But seems younger – you should have seen him blush! He told

53

me he's to carry the regimental colours and seemed so proud. I'm going to keep as far away from Moffat as possible. You haven't seen Lieutenant Kincaid, have you?'

I recollected seeing a very tall man in a dark-green uniform hurtling towards the beeches and indicated the direction.

'If I'm going to be caught by anyone I'd rather it was Kincaid – or Charles Croft.'

She ran off the way I had pointed out.

I suddenly found Sir Henry at my elbow and gave an exclamation of surprise.

'You startled me!'

'I'm sorry.'

'No, I'm glad to see you. I think I've had enough. I've no breath left.'

'Nor have I. Shall we walk a little and cool down?'

It was very agreeable, walking beneath the beeches with the sun filtering through the leaves. He made me take his arm when the ground became uneven and we chatted in a desultory fashion like old friends. He told me about his home in Dorset and how he hoped one day to restore it.

'I've nothing very grand in mind, but if I could mend the roof, repair the windows and get everything into decent order . . . but I fear it is hopeless. I don't think Charles's solution of marrying a rich widow would do the trick.'

'Oh, what a pity! I thought you might carry off Lady Silbury.'

He laughed. 'She'd frighten me to death!'

'Then her daughter. Isn't she an only child? An heiress?'

'Which no doubt explains why your cousin is pursuing her – or am I unduly cynical?'

'Not at all. There's also Ben's snobbery. He's always thought he was too good for us.'

We found ourselves looking down a bank on to the road, which was well paved with a ditch on either side.

'Well, at least we know where we are,' he said.

'There's a village called Waterloo a couple of miles down there and a crossroads. I rode down there with Charles one day. Nothing of any great interest as far as I could tell.'

We found our way back to the site of the picnic. Some of the party were still missing; others were quenching their thirst and laughing. Ben and Lydia had not yet returned, but Mrs Moffat had wakened and was demanding to know the whereabouts of her spouse.

Gradually everyone came back. Ben and Lydia were gazing into each other's eyes in a very silly way.

'That poor girl! ' I said. 'She doesn't know what he's really like.'

'It's foolish at this time to become too attached to a soldier,' said Sir Henry. 'The future is so precarious.'

I don't know if what happened next was entirely due to his words, but I had been conscious for the last few minutes of a growing unease. I am not unduly fanciful and I had never before experienced anything similar, but I was filled with an overwhelming sense of impending tragedy. It came now, as I looked at all those young officers with their fresh, sunburnt faces, so carefree and cheerful. It was as though a cloud had crossed the sun, but the cloud was inside my head.

'What's the matter?' my companion enquired. 'You've gone quite pale. Do you feel ill?'

'Not really. I was suddenly filled with sorrow at the thought of those young men going off to war – some of them not coming back, some with horrible wounds. . . .'

'It's best not to think of it. Many of them have been through it before. They don't let it oppress them or they wouldn't be much use in the army.'

I shivered and then the horror had gone.

On the journey home the officers burst into song – mostly ditties popular with the army: 'The Girl I Left Behind Me' and 'The British Grenadiers'.

Mrs Moffat looked disapproving. 'It ill behoves these young men to be so frivolous when they may be facing death in the next few weeks. "In that day the Lord will punish with his sword, his fierce, great and powerful sword, Leviathan, the gliding serpent." They should be singing hymns.'

'The Prussians sing hymns quite beautifully,' I pointed out, 'but the Belgians don't like them because they treat them badly and take whatever they want without paying. They prefer our men because they are polite and well behaved and pay for everything.'

Suddenly the officers began singing 'Over the Hills and Far Away'. I had always thought the words and tune curiously affecting. I found myself close to tears. 'If I should fall to rise no more, as many comrades did before . . .' sang Charles, with a cheerful grin on his face.

'You look very melancholy, Elizabeth,' said Sir Henry, coming closer to the carriage.

'It's nothing. I find that song so sad.'

'So do I. It reminds me of when Charles was in the Peninsula and I never knew if he'd be coming home.'

'How many of these will be coming home?'

'That only time will tell.'

It was only afterwards that I realised he had called me by my Christian name for the first time.

When we reached the hotel, Carrie and I went straight to my uncle and aunt's room to tell them about our day.

The Crofts and the Moffats went on ahead of us to the third floor. I don't know what happened to Ben; I think he had escorted the Silburys to their hotel.

It wasn't until my cousin and I continued our climb to our own room that we became aware of a commotion: shouting, sobs, wailing, and other voices trying to restore calm. We soon found out what was wrong when we saw Mr Moffat at the open door of his room, proclaiming that he had been burgled and all his wife's jewels stolen.

CHAPTER NINE

Mr Moffat was holding forth to an interested audience of hotel guests, including the Crofts and the two officers who shared Ben's room. The Moffats' door stood open and I could see Mrs Moffat sobbing in the armchair, which she overlapped alarmingly. I went in to her and offered her my smelling salts, which she almost snatched from my hand. Unable to speak, she pointed to the bed where a jewel box lay on its side.

On glancing round the room, I could see no other disturbance. Obviously the jewel thief had wanted only one thing. Then I looked more closely. A valise in a corner of the room stood open. Perhaps it was like that before the Moffats left for the picnic, or the thief had opened it to see if it contained anything of value.

'No!' I heard Mr Moffat exclaiming. 'Only jewels. He left some money in a drawer.'

'Foolish to leave anything of value in a hotel,' said someone.

'Was the door forced or unlocked?' I heard Henry Croft's voice.

'What? Oh – no – I unlocked it when we returned. Someone must have had a key.'

'Or the means of turning a lock,' said Charles. 'A skeleton key of some sort.'

'Were they the jewels my uncle valued for you?' I whispered to Mr Moffat.

'Yes, of course they were. A few other items were left behind – lockets and chains and so forth. Does Mr Wakefield know anything about it?'

'I doubt it, but you can ask him yourself.'

'I think we'd better send for the proprietor,' said Sir Henry. 'The local police should be informed.'

It seemed to me that Mr Moffat was not entirely taken with the idea.

'Lay not up for yourselves treasures on earth where thieves break through and steal,' groaned his wife.

He turned on her irritably. 'For heaven's sake hold your tongue, you stupid woman! Who wants to hear your sanctimonious maundering?'

'Ah!' I thought. 'He's showing his true colours now.'

Madame Dubois was horrified and regarded the theft as a reflection on the respectability of her hotel. Monsieur Dubois would be equally shocked, she assured us, and he'd insist on calling the police. Mr Moffat did not seem to be entirely happy with the idea, but eventually a rather dull officer arrived, and, with Madame Dubois as interpreter, asked a few questions, made a few laborious notes and then departed. He suggested that with so many foreign soldiers in the city and war imminent it would be very difficult to pursue any sort of inquiry, but if the Moffats made out a detailed list of the items missing he would circulate it among the local jewellers.

When I told my uncle of these events he said that Moffat had not been to see him.

'I suspect our friend does not want a too rigorous investigation. I've always thought there was something suspicious about those jewels.'

'You think they belong to Lady Silbury?'

'I'd not be at all surprised if they're safely back in her jewel case. I doubt if she'll wear them as long as the Moffats are in Brussels, but I don't think this was a theft so much as a restoration of property. I don't think Moffat actually stole them.'

'He got hold of them by issuing threats of some sort?'

'Yes, and we may not have seen the end of it.'

But greater events soon intervened. The theft of a few jewels, however valuable, seemed trivial compared with what lay in wait for us.

The next few days passed in a dream. There remained with me an underlying sense of foreboding, which increased the desire for pleasure. Carrie and I managed to persuade Ben to escort us to the theatre and opera and we grew quite reckless about walking in the park unchaperoned, usually in the company of Henry and Charles Croft. The former had become a firm friend, and I had begun to hope for more. Charles I loved as a sister loves a brother. Carrie was enchanted by him and prattled away merrily, reducing him to helpless laughter with her quips. When the army moved on, and that day seemed rapidly approaching, the little flirtation would come to an end.

On the brilliant, sunny morning of the 15th of June, Carrie and I went shopping for lace. As we came out of the shop we encountered Mr Kean, who was coming out of the draper's next door with a bolt of linen under his arm.

'Not much left,' he said. 'I'm lucky to get this. A lot of officers have been buying it.'

'But why?' asked Carrie.

'To make bandages, of course – there are never enough. It won't be long now; I've been sharpening my instruments.'

I suppressed a shudder. The sunlight suddenly seemed dimmed.

'I'm taking this back to the hotel and then I'll see how your mother is getting on,' he told Carrie.

We went on to the park, which was, as usual, filled with soldiers in colourful uniforms strolling along the paths, many of them with muslin-clad girls on their arms.

'It doesn't seem possible,' said Carrie. 'Everything is so calm and cheerful.'

'Good morning, young ladies!' an all-too-familiar voice called out behind us, and we turned to see the Moffats approaching.

Carrie groaned and I felt equally annoyed.

'So nice to meet you, isn't it, Phoebe?'

Mrs Moffat grunted in reply, but did not look too pleased.

'I expect you've heard of the great ball the Duchess of Richmond is giving tonight? Lady Silbury and her daughter are going, of course, and everyone else of note in noble and military circles. The Croft brothers have been invited as they are gentry, though impoverished, and their father was a friend of the Duke of Richmond. I don't suppose they'll go as they don't mix much in society.

'At all events this should scotch the rumours about Boney entering Belgium. I'm sure the Duke would not let it go ahead if there was the slightest possibility of an attack,' Mr Moffat continued.

'We saw Mr Kean buying linen for bandages this morning,' said Carrie. 'He thinks a battle is coming,'

'He can't be far wrong, but nobody knows exactly when. We'll be perfectly safe here. The French will never get to Brussels. '

At that moment we saw Mr Fox sitting on one of the benches smoking his clay pipe. He smiled and raised his hat to us as we passed by.

'Do you know that man?' enquired Mr Moffat.

'No, not really,' I replied, 'but I've seen him about and he's spoken to me once or twice. He lodges near our hotel.'

'He was at the review; he's everywhere. I fear he's a criminal. It wouldn't surprise me if he was the thief who stole Phoebe's jewellery.'

'Really? He didn't strike me as belonging to the criminal classes,' I said.

'And what can you know of them, my dear young lady? Nothing, I hope.'

I was wondering desperately how we could escape from our unwanted companions when Mrs Moffat, who was very red in the face, and fanning herself vigorously, complained of feeling the heat.

'Those steps at the hotel don't help. I'm tired before we come out,' she said.

A vacant bench was found and we made our excuses and left them, saying we were going to the pavilion for lemonade. We hastened away before they could ask us to bring them some

'I don't want to go back to the hotel yet,' said Carrie. 'It's so hot and stuffy indoors and I'm tired of reading to Mama and listening to her complaints. It's lovely here under the trees.'

'But your poor father has been sitting with her all morning. We ought to relieve him.'

She shrugged. 'He can always leave Molly with Mama.'

'The company of a maid is not—'

'Oh, do stop objecting, Lizzie. I've noticed Ben avoids anything at all tiresome. He doesn't have many duties, but he's never available to take his turn with us.'

'True! He's more interested in courting Lydia Silbury and telling lies about his family.'

'Ought we to tell them the truth? That would put an end to his ambitions.'

'No, not yet. We'll keep that in reserve. It may be useful to save it as a threat.'

Carrie giggled. 'Sometimes you are very *sly*, Lizzie.'

'Sometimes one needs to be.'

We compromised in the end and stayed in the park until after two. Then we returned to the hotel, where we found both my aunt and my uncle fast asleep.

At dinner that afternoon Ben had been persuaded, with one or two veiled threats, to join Carrie and me. Uncle Nat now always dined with Aunt Hetty in their room.

I noticed the absence of the Croft brothers and supposed they were dining elsewhere, but they entered just as we were about to leave.

'We thought you'd like to hear the latest news,' said Charles. 'The Prussians are engaged with the French near Charleroi, so Boney is in Belgium and heading this way.'

'I heard something of the sort in a coffee house before I came here,' said Ben, 'but I didn't believe it. There have been so many rumours.'

'This is true enough,' said Charles. 'I had it from Major Wylie, who'd come straight from the Duke. The news was brought in while he was there. Lord Wellington is waiting for further news from Blücher before making any decisions.'

'We're going to the Richmond ball,' said Sir Henry. 'It's not entirely my sort of thing, but anyone who is anyone will be there, including the Duke, so we should find out exactly what's going on.'

Later I saw them leave for the ball, Sir Henry in elegant evening dress and Charles resplendent in his finest uniform.

Carrie seemed very nervous, especially as we had heard that many English people were planning to leave Brussels if Bonaparte came any nearer.

'We can't go, whatever happens,' I told her. 'Your mother can't be moved – your father won't leave without her and I'm sure you won't either.'

'No, of course not,' she said, but she still looked troubled.

CHAPTER TEN

In the earlier part of the evening I was alone in my room as Carrie had gone to join her parents. Ben had departed heaven knows where with a few of his cronies. I tried to read, but absorbed nothing as my mind was continually wandering, my ears listening for anything unusual, either in the hotel or in the street outside. It was a hot evening and I sat near the open window trying to find a little fresh air. The street seemed busier than usual with hordes of people, mostly military, heading in the direction of the Place Royale.

It was long after dark when I heard footsteps bounding up the stairs and along the corridor past my room. Somebody was hammering loudly on the Crofts' door and shouting, 'Charlie! Charlie!'

I peeped out, and by the light of the candle sconce on the wall I saw a tall figure in Rifle green. It was Charles Croft's friend Johnny Kincaid. At once I went out to him.

'They aren't here,' I explained. 'They've gone to the Duchess of Richmond's ball.'

'The devil they have!' He was still somewhat out of breath from having charged up the hundred steps.

'They went to find out more about the present situation. I'm sure they won't stay there long.'

'Could you give Charles a message from me?'

'Of course.'

'Tell him to pack his traps as soon as possible and get his baggage animals ready to march at dawn. I met one of the Duke's staff in the park this evening and he asked me if my packsaddles were ready. I said nearly so, but surely they wouldn't be needed before tomorrow. He advised me not to delay so long.

'I'm in the Place Royale with my men. Tell Charlie to join me as soon as possible. I've been trying to get some rest, but it's hopeless. The pavement's confounded hard to start with, but people keep falling over me and asking what's going on. I was just drifting off at one point when that tiresome little busybody who was at the picnic – Muffin or Muffler or some such name – woke me up, telling me I ought not to be sleeping when Boney was about to attack. I advised him to keep calm and go home to bed – if he didn't want to take my place. I must go – there are one or two other friends I want to find. There's no point trying to rest. Goodbye! I hope we meet again.'

'So do I.' I took his hand in mine. 'Good luck and God bless you!'

'Yes, I could do with that.' He kissed my hand hastily and ran back to the head of the stairs.

I turned just in time to see the door next to mine about to close.

'Ah, Mrs Moffat!' I cried. 'Isn't your husband with you?'

'He's gone out to see what information he can obtain. He thinks we may have to make a hasty departure. What *did* that impertinent young man want?'

'Oh, didn't you hear?'

She bridled. 'I'm entitled to know what's going on.'

'Lieutenant Kincaid is ready to march at dawn, so presumably action is expected very soon.'

'You think the army will leave us here? Who will protect us?'

'They're hardly likely to fight a battle here in Brussels. They'll march to meet Bonaparte.'

'That man will have much to answer for at the great Day of Judgement.'

'I daresay.'

'The man who made the world a desert, who overthrew its cities . . .'

'Indeed!'

She closed the door.

I went into my room, even more restless, wishing the Croft

brothers would return so that I could ask them what was happening. Soon afterwards Carrie came in, flushed and breathless after her climb upstairs, and looking rather cross.

'Papa wants to go out to discover what's going on,' she said. 'But he wants you to go with him because you speak French. I reminded him I speak French too, but he just laughed and said that no foreigners seemed to understand me. I think they just pretend not to know what I'm saying to be awkward. Are the Crofts back yet?'

'No, I wasn't expecting them until midnight at the earliest. Lieutenant Kincaid called to tell Charles to get ready to move out. The 95th Rifles are assembling in the Place Royale.'

'This is dreadful! I never thought we'd be trapped like this. I wish we'd all stayed at home.'

'We're not trapped and I'm going out.'

I found a bonnet and a light shawl and we set off downstairs to where my uncle was waiting for me. Carrie went in to her mother looking rather sulky.

As we left the hotel we were joined by Mr Kean, the former naval surgeon.

'Do you mind if I accompany you?' he asked. 'I've a little French, so I may be of some use.'

'That's why I brought Elizabeth along,' said Uncle Nat. 'She speaks good French and she's been invaluable while we've been here. I wish sometimes we'd never come, though I'm sure Bonaparte will soon be defeated.'

'I believe Moffat's been scurrying round like a mad rabbit,' said Mr Kean with a grin.

I didn't repeat what Johnny Kincaid had told me.

The street seemed to be full of soldiers and there was much banging on doors and shouting. As we reached the vast expanse of the Place Royale we saw the military massing in large numbers, together with horses and baggage wagons. The air was filled with bugle calls and bellowed orders. We moved on to the park, but found the gates locked for the evening. There was an undercurrent of excitement and anticipation.

'They're getting ready to move out,' observed Mr Kean.

'Marching at dawn, I shouldn't wonder.'

'My son will be going. I wonder where he is.' My uncle sounded troubled.

I realised this was why we were wandering round Brussels after dark on the eve of war. Occasionally we stopped some soldier and asked the whereabouts of Ben's regiment. When we tracked them down, the soldiers claimed not to know where Lieutenant Wakefield might be. Not all the officers had appeared, however, as they were scattered throughout the city.

I was very touched by the sight of soldiers saying farewell to their wives, often with small children clinging to their necks. I remembered the poor dead woman in the park and wondered if the husband she sought was among the multitude preparing to march. Did he know she was dead and would never welcome him home if he survived? Did he know only too well that she was dead because he had killed her? The question would probably never be answered, I thought.

Eventually we returned to the hotel just in time to see the two officers who shared Ben's room leaving through the front door.

'Oh, he's still inside,' said young Parker in answer to my uncle's inquiry. 'He's saying goodbye to his mother and said he'll join us later.' Parker's round schoolboy face was flushed with excitement.

'Did you know I was carrying the colours?' he asked. 'It's a great honour.'

'Yes, Carrie told me.'

'Give her my l— regards, and tell her I'll bring her an eagle.'

Behind him Lieutenant Hayward looked grave and shook his head.

'Curb your enthusiasm, lad. Carrying the colours is confounded dangerous.'

But little Parker refused to be suppressed and went on his way whistling merrily.

There was a tearful scene being acted out in my uncle and aunt's room, with Carrie in floods of tears and Aunt Hetty clinging round Ben's neck and begging him not to go. This I thought ridiculous; it was like imploring him to desert. As my uncle went in I slipped away. I felt I had no part to play in this particular drama. I was sure Ben had no wish to embrace me, and the distaste was mutual.

I was very tired and the climb to my room seemed particularly wearisome, especially as officers and their servants were clattering downstairs laden with luggage and equipment and drawing to one side to let me pass. When I reached the third floor I found the Croft bothers had returned from the Duchess of Richmond's ball and Charles was ready to leave. I told them of Kincaid's visit, but they already knew the full story.

'While we were at the ball we heard the worst news confirmed. Blücher's Prussians have been driven back and our army is setting out at dawn to intercept the French advance on Brussels.'

'Some of the officers stayed on to enjoy the ball,' added Charles. 'They'll end up wearing their dancing shoes on the battlefield. They had permission to stay on till dawn, provided they joined their regiments later. Most of us came away.'

I noticed he had changed into an old, shabby uniform. His servant and Dobbs were heaving baggage about and went off downstairs fully loaded.

Beyond the window the clamour of a gathering army rose on the mild night air: the clatter of hooves, the rumble of wagons, the babble of voices, shouted orders and the call of a bugle, repeated like a distant melancholy echo in different parts of the city. Another sound, wild and blood-curdling, was adding its dismal wail to the tumult below.

'The pipes,' smiled Charles, 'not a cat being strangled. Just the Highlanders preparing for battle.'

'There's no need for you to go yet,' said Sir Henry. 'Why not rest here for an hour or two? You'd be more comfortable.'

'I'd rather be with my men.'

'As you wish. Goodbye, and good fortune!' The two brothers clasped hands.

For once Charles looked perfectly serious. 'Yes, I've an idea I shall need it. Well, this is the first time I've taken leave of you directly before going into action, and, to tell the truth, I'd rather you weren't here. Don't come down with me. Goodbye, dear Hal!'

He took a few steps down the corridor and saw me hovering uncertainly at the door of my room.

'Elizabeth,' he said, 'do you think you could do something for me?'

'I'm sure I'd like to.'

'Would you mind kissing me goodbye? It may be the last time.'

'Of course,' I said.

The kiss was warm but gentle. He thanked me hoarsely, then he left without a backward glance. The door to his room closed softly and I realised Sir Henry had heard us.

CHAPTER ELEVEN

I slept little that night. Carrie joined me looking cross and sullen, her face still smudged with tears, her irritability masking her nervousness. I pretended an insouciance I was far from feeling.

'You didn't say goodbye to Ben!' she said accusingly.

'I thought he had enough to cope with: two weeping women and an anxious father. He wouldn't want my farewells anyway.'

No, I thought, the kiss I exchanged with Charles Croft was worth a hundred perfunctory pecks on the cheek from a reluctant Ben.

We were preparing to go to bed when there was a knock at the door and we heard Mr Moffat's voice informing us that he had news that we might wish to hear. We put on our dressing gowns and went to find out what he had to say.

'I thought you might like to hear what I gleaned on my perambulations,' he began importantly.

'The French have taken Charleroi and driven back the Prussians. Bonaparte is at the head of an army said to be 200,000-strong. He is heading for Brussels.'

'What will become of us?' sobbed Carrie.

'Our army is in his way,' I said. 'I presume they will stop him.'

'Ah, but half our best soldiers are in America. The Duke of Wellington has to make do with Belgians and Dutch to fill in the gaps in his old Peninsular Army.'

'Which has never been beaten by the French.' I was determined to hope for the best, although I secretly felt anything but sanguine.

'You must be ready to flee the city at a moment's notice,' he continued. 'I fear for the fate of young girls like you. It's bad enough for the men, who are likely to be shot or taken prisoner if Boney comes here.'

'We can't leave. My aunt cannot be moved and we are not going to abandon her.'

'Ah, you are either blindly devoted or just plain foolish, I'm afraid. I bid you both goodnight. You know where I am if you require assistance.' With that he departed.

Carrie dissolved into tears again.

'Crying won't help,' I snapped, losing patience with her continual snivelling. 'The night is half over anyway. Perhaps we'll hear more cheerful news tomorrow.'

I lay down on my bed, but the night was hot and sultry with the promise of thunder. Even without the sounds of an army on the march it would have been difficult to sleep, though Carrie, it seemed, managed to doze fitfully. At last I rose and sat by the open window.

The sounds continued for a time: drumbeats, bugle calls, bagpipes, hoof beats, the rumble of gun carriages and wagons, endless shouting and marching feet. Gradually they faded away to be replaced by a heavy, sinister silence. The dawn promised another bright, warm summer morning.

Carrie and I breakfasted in the hotel dining room as usual, Uncle Nat staying upstairs with my aunt. It seemed almost deserted as all the officers had gone and so had a number of the civilians. Mr Kean asked permission to join us, and I was rather glad of his company as he seemed a sensible, practical man and not given to spreading wild rumours or instilling terror into poor Carrie.

'What are you going to do this morning?' he enquired.

'Mr Moffat says we ought to leave the city as soon as possible,' said Carrie.

'No doubt many would agree with him, but you cannot leave your mother.'

'I suppose not.'

'It might well impede her recovery if she attempted to travel to Antwerp, and what would she do when she got there? I really don't believe there is any immediate danger. Would you let me accompany you on a morning walk? Perhaps we may find out a little more.'

We agreed readily enough as the Moffats entered the room at that moment and we were afraid they might want to come with us.

'Then, let's go,' said Mr Kean. 'We'll send a message up to Mr & Mrs Wakefield, telling them we hope to bring back more news.'

Brussels had changed overnight. The city was deserted and had taken on a melancholy, forsaken atmosphere. People wandered the streets listlessly, stopping complete strangers to ask for information. We were almost amused to see a long string of carts bringing fruit and vegetables to the market. The more mundane aspects of life seemed to be going on as usual.

We caught sight of General Picton, still in civilian dress, riding out with a telescope slung over his shoulder and accompanied by his staff. He looked very grim. A passer-by told us he had seen the Duke of Wellington leaving at eight that morning.

There seemed little more to discover, so we returned to the hotel and I went up to my aunt and uncle. The first was still inclined to weep copiously, not having got over her beloved Benjie's departure.

'I don't want to go out again,' said Carrie. 'It's too depressing. Not a uniform in sight and everyone looking so gloomy and anxious. The print shops have taken all the caricatures of Bonaparte out of the windows, and someone told us there were a lot of Bonaparte's supporters in the city who've been lying low until now but they're planning a magnificent banquet to welcome him.'

'Pah!' said Uncle Nat. 'Tittle-tattle! There are bound to be people of that persuasion in every town – hoping to benefit from the imperial purse, I suppose.'

My uncle was rather irritable – the result, I supposed, of being cooped up for so long with my lachrymose aunt. I was not altogether surprised when, in the afternoon, he suggested we two should go out in the streets again to see if any news was available.

'Perhaps there'll be more to hear since you went out this morning, Lizzie, and I need you because you speak French.'

Carrie did not seem to mind greatly being left with her mother, although she had complained about it on previous occasions.

'Anything is better than seeing the Place Royale empty and miserable faces everywhere.'

Uncle Nat and I walked until we were tired, gathering conflicting rumours everywhere. Eventually we went into the park and, as neither of us felt like going back to the hotel, we bought refreshments at the pavilion and then found a bench to sit on.

We were remarking on the dismal aspect of the park now all the soldiers had departed, when we heard a distant rumbling sound.

'Thunder!' said my uncle. 'Only to be expected after all this hot weather. I haven't seen any lightning yet, have you?'

But the rumbling continued. People rose from their seats and pedestrians quickened their paces. Everyone headed towards the ramparts of the city facing south by the Namur Gate. We followed them; my uncle's interpretation of the sounds was now obviously wrong.

'A cannonade!' someone said.

'That's obvious!' another English voice replied. 'But where? A battle for sure, but how far away?'

We stayed on, desperate for news, but when it came it was contradictory, by turns hopeful and horrifying. The French had been defeated with 20,000 dead; the French had been victorious and were advancing on Brussels; Blücher had defeated the French; the Allies were vanquished and in retreat.

'Better not tell your aunt any of this,' said Uncle Nat, looking very anxious, his normally ruddy cheeks quite pale.

At about five o'clock the first wounded arrived and everyone rushed to the gate to see them enter on farm carts and ammunition wagons.

Those casualties who could still speak told us the situation was very bad and likely to get worse. No one seemed able to supply any convincing information.

We made our way back to the hotel in a dismal frame of mind, passing some of the wounded on our way. We heard the hospital was already full and other buildings were being hastily prepared to receive casualties. Some men managed to return to their billets, but others lay in the street, unable to go any further.

Several of the 92nd Gordon Highlanders were lying on the

pavement, dirty and dishevelled. I saw Mr Kean leaning over one of them, bandaging his leg. He glanced up at us.

'It's going to get worse,' he said. 'This is only the beginning.'

'I want to help,' I said.

'A number of the local ladies are taking round food and wine and trying to make the injured more comfortable,' he said. 'And you could scrape lint if I gave you some of that linen I bought.'

'Carrie can scrape lint and I'll take round refreshments, but I want to help in other ways – perhaps I could dress minor wounds.'

'I'd enjoy being bandaged by this young lady,' grinned the soldier with the injured leg, his teeth gleaming white in his dirty face.

'I'm sure you would, but you've missed your chance. I don't think you're going to lose that limb, but we'll have to keep an eye on it,' said Mr Kean.

My uncle asked the soldier a few questions, but the man shook his head.

'I don't know much more than you, sir – a battlefield's a confusing place. You can't see much because of the smoke. I only know it was bad – worse than anything I've ever known. Our colonel's been shot and the Duke was nearly captured. He got too near the enemy and they'd have caught him if he hadn't leapt his horse over the ditch we were in – fixed bayonets and all.'

'He takes too many risks,' said Uncle Nat, shaking his head.

'If you really want to help me,' said Mr Kean quietly, 'take my advice and go round the wounded with food and drink. They need it. Accustom yourself to seeing wounds. Later on we'll see if you can do more.'

My uncle usually let me have my way. There were already many women, some of them quite young and unaccompanied, taking water and brandy to the wounded and even cushions and blankets to ease the discomfort of those lying on cobbles.

I obtained a basket from the hotel kitchen and Madame Dubois was eager to help. She filled it with refreshments of every kind.

'I'd come with you,' she said, 'but I have too many duties here.'

I went out into the street and gave what help I could to the men lying there. Mr Kean was still attending to injuries in that brisk, professional way of his. I reflected that the navy had lost a good surgeon.

During the next hour I saw many horrible sights and forced myself to look and overcome nausea, telling myself that if I was to be of any use I had to grow accustomed to such things.

Although I was vaguely conscious of passers-by, I paid them little attention until a familiar voice spoke to me.

'You are doing admirable work, Miss Aston. May I help you?'

It was Henry Croft, astride his Flemish horse. He dismounted, took the basket, which was quite heavy, and carried it until we ran out of supplies.

'I rode out along the road from the Namur Gate to see if I could learn anything useful,' he told me. 'I passed many of the wounded. It seems there's been a battle at Quatre Bras, which is about twenty-five miles away. The Duke of Brunswick has been killed and things seem pretty bad. Our army is withdrawing to keep in touch with the Prussians.'

He laid his hand on my arm so that I had to look him in the face.

'Elizabeth, I understand you and your cousin cannot leave the city because of Mrs Wakefield's injury. I will look after you both as best I can, I promise you that.'

I thanked him, noting his serious, anxious expression and realised he was worrying over us as well as his brother.

When I retired that night it occurred to me that I did not think of Ben, but only of Charles Croft and his friend Kincaid and Hayward and little Parker and the other officers at the picnic.

I slept soundly, exhausted by the previous sleepless night and the exertions of the day. In the early morning I was woken by the hotel servants screaming that the French were at the gates of the city.

A chambermaid pounded on the door.

'Les Français sont ici!' she shrieked.

'It's all over,' sobbed Carrie. 'We're all going to die – or worse!'

CHAPTER TWELVE

I threw on my dressing gown and rushed to the door, closely followed by my terrified cousin. From the shouts and screams and clattering I expected to see signs of confusion, but nothing prepared me for the seething mass of humanity in various stages of undress, struggling along the passage and down the stairs, impeded by people who were trying to get back to their rooms for items they had forgotten.

As I stood hesitating, scarcely able to move from my doorway for fear of being knocked down, I found myself seized round the waist in a firm grip and pulled back against a man who had stopped directly behind me.

'Don't get caught up in that mob,' said a voice in my ear. 'I'll see you come to no harm.' It was Sir Henry Croft in his dressing gown.

'Are the French really here?'

'Of course not, but there's hysteria in the air. Everyone's going down to try and secure horses. I'll make damned sure they don't get hold of mine. I advise you to go back in and lock the door.'

'But I wanted to go to my aunt and uncle. They'll be so alarmed.'

'In that case I'll see you safely down. Miss Wakefield,' he shouted to the shivering Carrie, 'there's no need for alarm; the French are miles away. I'm taking your cousin to see your parents. Lock yourself in until she comes back.'

The next door opened and Mr Moffat's head, in a red nightcap, viewed the turmoil with consternation. Behind him I saw the head of his wife, adorned with curlpapers, her jaws wobbling.

'Ah!' observed Mr Moffat, 'I see, Miss Aston, that you have already obtained assistance. What has happened to your cousin?'

'Miss Wakefield is safely locked in her room,' Sir Henry replied. 'I've told her to stay there. This is a false alarm started by hysterical servants. Go back to bed.'

All the time I was conscious of my back pressing against his chest, a circumstance I found both comforting and disturbing. In our nightclothes too! Back in England it would be enough to cause a scandal, but here, among the panics of war, it was nothing out of the ordinary at all.

'Woe!' moaned Mrs Moffat. 'Woe, o great city! In one hour your doom has come!'

'Oh, do be quiet, Phoebe!' snapped her unsympathetic spouse.

'I'm sure that referred to Babylon,' said Sir Henry, 'but in any case we are far from doomed. Please go back to bed – there's nothing to be gained from joining this stampede.'

We left them to their own devices and began to push our way downstairs. I found my aunt in tears and my uncle greatly agitated. Sir Henry came in to reassure them and they seemed to calm down a little.

I was surprised to find Mr Kean already there, a shabby naval greatcoat over his shirt. Sir Henry glanced at him and gave him a brusque nod before continuing his attempt to make sure his horse was secure.

'I came down at once to see that your aunt was safe,' Mr Kean told me, 'and to make sure no attempt was made to move her. There is no real danger. She is much safer here than jolting in a coach to Antwerp or wherever the idiots are all fleeing. That's if you could get transport, which I doubt.'

'It's nice to know these gentlemen are so concerned for our welfare,' said Uncle Nat. 'Your aunt's been very frightened.'

'So has everyone, I think,' I said, 'but I'm sure it's a false alarm. We'll find out more tomorrow.'

'I'd rather stay here anyway,' said Aunt Hetty bravely. 'I couldn't face another journey with this leg. I'm closer to Benjie here and I'm sure the Duke is to be relied on.'

Sir Henry came back twenty minutes later to announce there

had almost been a riot in the stables with people desperate for horses to take them away from the city.

'I left Dobbs there to keep an eye on my horse and I gave him my pistol to show a little determination if so required. I paid a hefty lad to stay with him till everything's calmed down. The panic seems to be subsiding already, so try to rest for another hour or two.'

He then escorted me to my room. Carrie was red-faced and furious.

'Why did you abandon me? Where have you been?'

'With your parents – you knew that. It was not at all pleasant being jostled and pushed about on the stairs. If Sir Henry hadn't escorted me I doubt if I'd have got down safely. We can go back to bed now for a while.'

Carrie, however, remained agitated and after breakfast refused to leave the hotel but stayed with her mother while I went out with Uncle Nat to see what information we could obtain.

As we turned into the Place Royale we saw the Moffats hastening along ahead of us, Mr Moffat carrying a small valise. His wife seemed to have trouble keeping up with him.

Outside the Hôtel Belle Vue stood an elegant barouche. Three ladies were climbing into it: Lady Silbury, her daughter and Miss Barlow, the companion. The English coachman was laying about him with his whip as people desperate for transport tried to seize the horses.

'Just in time!' cried Mr Moffat.

Lady Silbury leaned out. 'We do have room for one more lady.' She looked in my direction and beckoned.

My uncle pushed me forward. 'Go, my dear – don't lose the chance to escape.'

'No, I want to stay here with you. I'd never forgive myself if I deserted you.'

While I was remonstrating, Mr Moffat bundled his wife into the carriage.

'You must save yourself, my love – for my sake!'

Lady Silbury glared angrily at the unwanted addition to her party, but the coachman shouted that he must be off at once or he could not answer for the consequences. Mr Moffat threw up the valise and kissed his hand as the carriage set off with its female load.

'Thank heaven Phoebe will be safe. They are going to Antwerp, I believe. Such a relief to have her off my hands. A man can always look after himself. Have you heard the latest? The mayor has appealed for bedding and supplies for the wounded. They are still coming in through the Namur Gate. I think I'll go along now and see if any of the injured can give me news of the campaign. One hears such rumours.'

We were glad to see the back of him. I think we had both come to regard him as an irritation. In the middle of the morning we heard an official bulletin announcing a victory for our army at Quatre Bras, which was what Sir Henry had told me the previous day.

The streets were still full of wounded soldiers though they were gradually being removed to hospitals or taken in by local residents. We returned to the hotel and collected a basket of provisions, which my uncle helped me to distribute. I noticed he turned his head away from a few particularly distressing sights which I had already schooled myself to regard with a measure of self-control.

On the way back to the hotel we were informed by an agitated stranger that the British Army was in retreat, pursued by the French. We were further alarmed to find our street full of baggage wagons, which extended in a long line back to the park. They had apparently come in through the Namur Gate; obviously the army had sent its baggage to the rear.

My uncle asked one of the wagoners why they had returned to Brussels. He replied that they had been given orders to withdraw and wait until sent for.

'That's all I can tell you, sir. They don't explain anything to the likes of us.'

This served to increase our anxiety, but was nothing compared to the shock that awaited us when we entered our hotel. In my uncle's room we found Aunt Hetty accompanied only by Molly, the maid.

'Where's Carrie?' cried my aunt, who was obviously in a state of great agitation.

'We thought she was going to stay with you,' my uncle replied.

'She was to start with. Then she said she was going up to her room to fetch something, but she didn't come back. I thought she'd gone out to find you, even though she said she didn't want to leave the hotel.'

'We haven't seen her,' I said. 'Perhaps she's still in our room. We've had so many disturbed nights. Perhaps she's lying down asleep.'

'Yes, yes, of course,' said Aunt Hetty. 'I should have sent Molly, but I didn't want to be left alone.'

'I'll go up and see,' I volunteered, and as I ascended the stairs I encountered Mr Kean, who was coming down with his medical bag and a roll of linen.

'Ridiculous business, early this morning,' he remarked. 'I hope you and your cousin were not too inconvenienced.'

I explained to him what had happened and he at once offered to come upstairs with me. The room was empty, but showed signs of hasty packing. A scribbled note lay on the table.

'Forgive me, dear Lizzie – I can stand this horror no more. Convey my regrets to my parents. I am seeking a place of safety. CW.'

'But where can she possibly have gone on her own?' I wondered. 'It's so dangerous.'

'Perhaps someone offered her a lift to Antwerp.'

'Then why didn't she tell us? Her parents would at least have been reassured if she had gone with another family or a respectable lady.'

'I don't think that's what happened. Did you notice that the door next to yours is open? Isn't it occupied by those intolerable Moffats?'

I at once turned my attention to the neighbouring room. It showed the same signs of hasty packing as the one I had just left.

'I fear this is the answer,' he said, 'though I suppose Mrs

Moffat is a perfectly adequate chaperone.'

'No,' I said, and told him of the scene we had witnessed outside the Hôtel Belle Vue that morning.

'So if Mrs Moffat has gone off to Antwerp with Lady Silbury, where is her husband? Not heading in the same direction, I'll be bound. He must have secured transport somehow. He has money, I fancy. I've heard talk of twenty napoleons being offered for a horse.'

'My uncle and I heard of a hundred – but whatever Moffat's arranged, how are we to get my cousin back? For all her worldly airs she's really a little innocent.'

'A little idiot, more like, to commit herself to the care of a man like that. I suppose it may be possible among all the confusion to find out where they've gone, but I think it's a hopeless case.'

I was not cheered by his observations and saw no gentle way of breaking the news to my aunt and uncle, so I went downstairs again with Carrie's note and told them what had happened. Mr Kean went off on his errand of mercy and I could not help but admire his dedication.

'You must go out and look for her!' my aunt cried hysterically. 'She may not have gone far.'

'It's useless,' my uncle groaned. 'The whole city is in turmoil. Everyone is trying to get away. The roads are crowded with fugitives and we've no idea where they've gone.'

'Except that it's unlikely to be Antwerp as Mrs Moffat will be there,' I observed.

'Carrie tried to do something like this before,' sobbed Aunt Hetty. 'Remember how she tried to run off with that medical student?'

Which, I reflected, would have resulted in a hasty marriage and Carrie eventually becoming a respectable doctor's wife. This was far worse.

'At least make some effort to find her – you may discover *something*.'

Uncle Nat and I set out, not knowing where to go. I suddenly thought of Mr Fox, the ubiquitous man in the drab coat, who seemed to know everything about everyone. I recalled that the first time I had encountered him, on the packet boat, he had asked me if I knew Mr Moffat and later he seemed to be observing him. I told my uncle of this, and as we had to pass Mr Fox's lodgings we decided to call and see if his landlady could tell us of his whereabouts. By good fortune, while looking at the front of the house we saw Mr Fox at an open window in his shirtsleeves. He caught sight of us and leaned out.

'Anything I can do?' he enquired.

'I do hope so,' I said. 'Please come down, Mr Fox, so that we can talk to you.'

'No sooner said than done!'

In a very short time he came out of the door in his familiar drab coat, his black hat in his hands.

'This place seems empty without those Highlanders. I fear they met – or may meet – a sad end. Now tell me the problem.'

'In confidence,' said my uncle, 'in strictest confidence! My daughter's reputation depends upon it.'

Between us we told him the sorry story of Carrie's flight with Mr Moffat.

'They are sure to be together,' I added. 'He pushed his wife into Lady Silbury's carriage this morning and they went off to Antwerp, so we are sure they've not gone there. Ostend might be more likely.'

'Yes, indeed,' he agreed. 'The man is a rogue who lives by extorting money from people by the use of threats. His wife, I am sure, knows nothing of this – nor the fact that he still has a first wife elsewhere. The present Mrs Moffat has money and he'll only abandon her when he's spent it all. I've been keeping an eye on him for some time, in the service of a noble lady who was, and still is, his victim. I should explain – and this is in strictest confidence, as you say, exchanging one undertaking for another – that I am a law officer. We are allowed to take on private work from time to time.'

'You are a Bow Street Runner?' exclaimed my uncle delightedly.

'That's what the public call us, certainly. But I must be off. As there are two of them I imagine he's managed to procure a gig.

That seems his favourite form of transport. I have a horse hidden away, so I should be able to overtake them even if they've had a good start. Confound this man! He's a really slippery customer. He still has some documents belonging to my client and I'm sure he carries them on his person. Perhaps I'll be able to retrieve them. But I'll rescue your daughter, sir, never fear. I'll bring her back to you safe and sound.'

'Back to us?' Uncle Nat was flustered. 'But shall we be here? Do you know what is happening? We heard the French were in hot pursuit of our army?'

'Try not to be alarmed. The British Army has withdrawn to keep in touch with the Prussians. I have it on the best authority. There's a great conflict coming, probably tomorrow, but there's nothing we can do about it. I hope to restore your daughter to you before then. I must delay no longer.'

We thanked him profusely before he disappeared into the house.

'Do you think Lady Silbury is the lady who employs him?' said my uncle thoughtfully.

'I'm sure of it.'

'And I wouldn't be surprised if he stole her jewels back when you were all at the picnic.'

'Serve Moffat right!'

'I think we can trust Mr Fox, Lizzie, don't you?'

'Yes, certainly.'

'We can tell your aunt that we have an experienced officer of the law tracking down Carrie and her abductor.'

It was later I recollected what Mr Fox had said about the former wife of Mr Moffat and I shuddered. Had she come to Brussels in search of him, ready to denounce him to his present wife? And had he met her in the park and killed her in that secluded spot where we had found her? Was my dear, silly cousin in the hands of a murderer? I fancied our law-officer friend knew more than he was telling us.

There seemed little point in wandering the streets on our sore feet, so we returned to the hotel and told my aunt that the best possible person had set off in pursuit of the errant Carrie. She was relieved, but still wept.

'I thought I would be suffering anxiety for one of my children, but now it's for both.'

I felt sorry for her, but she would not be comforted.

That night there were thunderstorms and torrential rain. We all thought of the army, so near to us, huddled in the mud awaiting a great battle. We knew now that it was very close, both in time and place.

Gloom had darkened to a sense of dread. The heavy air and rumblings of thunder added to the apprehension. I thought the downpour might bring relief, but it somehow increased my anxiety. I could think of nothing but my friends in the Rifles and poor little Parker, out in the rain awaiting the possibility of death on the morrow. I scarcely gave Ben a thought, though I hoped he would survive for his parents' sake. A night in the rain would do him good. I later regretted these callous sentiments.

I lay down on my bed, fully dressed apart from my shoes, unable to sleep for the howling of the wind, the lashing of the rain and my own chaotic thoughts. Every now and then I rose and sat at the window, straining my ears and eyes until I was so exhausted that I threw myself down again and fell into a troubled slumber disturbed by hideous dreams.

CHAPTER THIRTEEN

The hotel seemed curiously empty the next morning. The officers had long since departed and the Moffats had left, together with many other guests. Mr Kean had gone out before breakfast.

My uncle and aunt were eating in their room as usual.

'I can't leave your aunt in this state,' Uncle Nat murmured, 'but I'd like to find out what's going on if you can find someone respectable to accompany you. The rumours are quite frightening and I don't want her to hear them. I'm sure they are totally misleading, but perhaps you will find the truth somewhere. If only our minds could be set at rest regarding Carrie. It's bad enough worrying about Ben.'

I went down to breakfast alone and was soon joined by Sir Henry Croft, looking even graver than usual, though he managed a rare smile when he greeted me. It was a relief to tell him about Carrie and he was very sympathetic.

'If that Fox fellow is a police officer he should know what he is doing. I'm sure that if he can't find them, then nobody can.'

Before I knew it I was telling him about the discovery of the murdered woman in the park.

'I'm so afraid it was Mr Moffat's real wife, and if so . . .'

'It must have been a great shock for you.'

'Yes, indeed, yet in retrospect it's the pathos I remember. She looked so poor yet so respectable. I recall her mended boots and her carefully darned gloves. How wicked to abandon a woman like that! At the time I promised not to tell and I still don't know if I did the right thing, but now Moffat's villainy has been exposed it hardly seems to matter, especially as we are surrounded by dead and dying with worse to come.'

Sir Henry had already been out early, seeking news.

'You can discount all the rumours,' he said. 'We are not in immediate danger, but there'll be an almighty battle today, that's for sure.'

'My uncle suggested I should go out and discover what's happening, if I can find a suitably respectable companion.'

'And you think I might be suitable,' he grinned. 'I'd be delighted. I doubt if we'll find out more than we know already, but we can hardly stay indoors in circumstances such as these.'

It was a dull, grey morning, the streets still wet from the previous night's rain. Heavy clouds still hung low in the sky, but at least the downpour had ceased. The city was in turmoil with people listlessly roaming about, begging everyone they met for information.

Later in the morning two things happened: the first seemed to auger well; the second filled us with apprehension. The wagons that filled the streets set off again, but where? Sir Henry shouted an enquiry.

'Namur Gate. We're rejoining the army.'

'It's all right.' Sir Henry squeezed my hand in the crook of his arm. 'If they'd been heading to Antwerp or Ostend I'd fear the worst, but they're going *towards* the action, not away from it.'

Shortly afterwards I heard what I supposed was a rumble of thunder, but it seemed infinitely prolonged and alarmingly close.

'A cannonade,' said my companion. 'Nearer than the one we heard on Friday – within ten miles perhaps.'

It continued without ceasing until it seemed as though we had never been without it: an incessant rumbling like someone rolling bowls down an uncarpeted staircase. We made our way to the ramparts, where many people were gathered, all intensely anxious and none very hopeful of the day's outcome.

'Can we follow after the wagons,' I suggested, 'and see if we can find out more at the Namur Gate?'

He agreed readily and we saw the last of the wagons depart down the road.

'We went along there on the day of the picnic,' I said. 'You told me it led eventually to a dull village called—'

'Waterloo,' he supplied. 'Yes, that would be about the right distance. A couple of miles further on there's a crossroads, open fields and a ridge. Charles said the Duke always likes to occupy a ridge and keep some of his men on the reverse slope until needed, out of the gunfire. Perhaps that's his game this time.'

We followed in the direction of the wagons, hoping to encounter someone coming from the battlefield. To our amazement we found many of the inhabitants of Brussels sitting at tables outside suburban inns and cafés, enjoying drinks and other refreshments as though it were a normal Sunday afternoon without the rumble of gunfire ten miles away. They chose to ignore it. One or two enquiries were met with a shrug. 'Whatever will be, will be' seemed to be the general attitude.

'How can they sit there drinking beer and smoking when so many good men are losing their lives so near at hand? Your poor brother!' I exclaimed.

'I know. It hardly seems right, but on the other hand you look very tired. I'm sure you've not been sleeping much. None of us has. Let's sit down and rest a while and I'll order coffee or lemonade. Then I'll take you home.'

It was a relief to agree to his suggestion as I was very weary. None of our neighbours seemed much concerned, not even when wagons arrived bearing the wounded. Sir Henry went to speak to some of them and came back shaking his head.

'They say things are very bad, but no one really knows what's going on as it's difficult to see very far. Charles told me how the gun smoke conceals everything unless the wind blows it away.' He looked very grim, but tried to smile at me. 'Poor girl, I think you've had enough. Let's go back to the hotel.'

It was on our way through the Place Royale that we encountered the worst alarm of the day. A large contingent of hussars galloped through yelling, *'Français! Français!'* and shouting in a mixture of French and German that the enemy were close behind.

As we had just returned from the Namur Gate, where there had been no sign of retreating or advancing troops, we knew this was a false alarm, but it caused me a momentary panic.

'German deserters!' pronounced my companion calmly. 'I doubt if the absence of such fellows will make much difference to the outcome of the battle.'

We walked home slowly; I was grateful for the support of his arm, and all I wanted to do now was lie on my bed for an hour or two. As we reached the door of the hotel we heard a loud shouting behind us from the square we had just left. Hastening back, our weariness forgotten, we saw a detachment of Horse Guards escorting a large number of French prisoners.

'Les Français sont ici after all,' said Sir Henry with a grin.

A little later an even larger number of prisoners arrived – near 5,000, we were told by a well-informed passer-by. When we expressed our delight he shook his head.

'I shouldn't count on it. Things are very bad. I hear Picton was killed leading his division. They say nothing can stop the French advance. I'm keeping a horse saddled and ready until I hear definite news.'

We returned to the hotel not knowing what to believe, but resolved not to say anything at all discouraging to my uncle and aunt. Sir Henry came into their room with me and a sorry sight met our eyes. Carrie, all travel-stained and bedraggled, her pelisse splashed with mud and her hair hanging limply out of curl, sprang to her feet as we entered.

'Thank heaven you're here!' she sobbed. 'They won't let me out of their sight. I've been sitting here since this morning – a *prisoner*!'

'You wicked girl!' cried Aunt Hetty. 'As if we haven't enough to worry about with poor Benjie in the heart of the battle. Running off with that odious Moffat! If it wasn't for that good Mr Fox you'd be in Ostend by now with your reputation ruined.'

'It wasn't like that. I was so frightened and he offered me a means of escape. I'm *still* frightened and nobody cares.' She sniffed into her handkerchief.

'We heard some shouting,' said Uncle Nat. 'What's going on?'

We told him all we knew, keeping our story as optimistic and encouraging as possible.

'You see!' Aunt Hetty directed a furious glance at her errant daughter. 'There was no need for you to run away at all. Our army will be victorious. We have the best of all commanders.'

'Please may I go up to my room now and wash and change?' begged Carrie. 'Lizzie can chaperone me?'

'I hope so,' said her mother. 'At least she's shown some fortitude and common sense.'

Aunt Hetty beckoned me over to her side. 'A word in your ear,' she whispered. 'Carrie has not told us everything that happened. Every time we pressed her she started crying. See if you can find out more – how that dreadful man treated her – you know what I mean.'

'I'll try,' I promised, 'but I don't know if she'll want to confide in me.'

Sir Henry escorted us back to our room.

'Have something to eat and then try to rest,' he advised. 'In an hour or two I'm going to ride through the Namur Gate towards the site of the battle. I'm sure it will be crowded with horses and vehicles, but I want to find my brother. If he's dead I want to search for his body; if he's wounded I need to make sure he's getting some attention and bring him back here if possible. I'm taking some water and brandy with me. I'm sure it will be needed.'

'It may be dangerous,' I protested.

'I have my pistols.'

'But suppose the worst has happened,' I whispered, glancing at Carrie. 'Suppose the French have won?'

'No one has won as long as we can hear that cannonade, and whatever the outcome I want to find Charles. I can't sit here waiting for news.'

'Then God help you!'

'God helps those who help themselves. Goodbye, my dear. I hope when we meet again we'll both be feeling a great deal happier. I'll also enquire after your brother, Miss Wakefield,' he added, addressing Carrie.

'Thank you. I fear it will be difficult among so many thousands.'

'Probably, but I will try.'

When he had gone Carrie gave me a sly look.

'You seem to have got very friendly with the baronet.'

'Not half as friendly as you and Mr Moffat. What *did* happen, Carrie?'

But Carrie was in no mood to answer, fussing about with the water jug.

'Ugh, no hot water. I don't suppose there's much use sending for any. Even if they have some they'll take ages to bring it up. Everything's so disorganised at the moment. And these silly little bowls hold next to nothing. Why can't they have proper basins?'

'You'll have to manage,' I told her unsympathetically.

She washed as well as she could, changed into another dress and brushed her hair, after which she said she felt much better.

'But I'm so tired. I had no sleep last night, jolting along that dreadful road with all that traffic and such tiresome people. I must have a rest. At least Mama let me have some tea.'

'I'm tired too, but I think you owe everyone an explanation after causing so much anxiety and heartache. What happened?'

'It was your fault, Lizzie. You shouldn't have left me alone in this room when I was so frightened. That was when I was determined to get away.'

'But I couldn't let you out into that mob on the stairs – you would have been hurt. It was a false alarm anyway.'

'I didn't know that. I only knew I couldn't stand any more of those terrors. Mr Moffat had always been kind, and with his wife gone he had only himself to consider.'

'Too kind, surely. I remember he tried to kiss you at the picnic and you were most annoyed.'

'Well, I just thought he was being silly. I didn't think it meant anything. I told him how frightened I was and he seemed so nice and helpful. He said he'd hired the gig and was keeping it in readiness. He'd spent twenty napoleons to secure it. His wife was supposed to go with him, but when the opportunity arose he thought she'd be safer with Lady Silbury so he had a spare seat and said he'd be glad to take me.'

'How could you be so naïve?'

'But he seemed like a friend and no one else seemed to care

what happened to me. We had only got as far as Ghent when that Fox man found us at an inn. He discovered Mr Moffat had secured one room only and intended us to share. Of course, the inn was very crowded and it may well have been the only room left, but. . . Oh, Lizzie, it was horrid! All the way to Ghent he was pressing himself against me and touching me and calling me his little darling. I felt sick!'

'He didn't attempt anything else — a real seduction? I'm sure you know what I mean.'

'How could he? We were in a gig on the open road with vehicles full of people trying to escape and others on horseback or on foot.'

'But what happened when Mr Fox found you? Where is Moffat now?'

'I don't know. He gave Mr Fox the slip – that is how he put it. He just ran off, upsetting tables and chairs and pushing people aside as he ran. By the time Mr Fox got outside he'd disappeared.'

'And Mr Fox brought you back in the gig?'

'Yes, leading his horse behind us. He had to beat off some dreadful ruffians who tried to seize the horses and he drew a pistol and threatened to shoot them. It was all so horrible!'

'You really were a fool, weren't you?'

'How was I to know what Moffat was planning?'

'It will be interesting to see what happens when his wife comes back from Antwerp.'

'That will only happen if all goes well. Oh, God, that endless rumbling like thunder! It's not knowing what's happening that makes it hard to bear?'

'I know, but we must be patient a little longer.'

We had no proper meals that day. A chambermaid knocked on the door and brought in a tray with slices of pie, salad and a carafe of wine. She explained that it was not worth opening the dining room. Few guests remained and the chef had fled, taking with him two of the kitchen menials. One of the maids had gone home to her mother, the bootboy was missing and Madame Dubois was frantic.

Carrie ate more than I could manage, but she had consumed

little in the last twenty-four hours. Afterwards we lay down in our clothes and slept.

When we woke the light was beginning to fade and we went to the open window and listened. There were a few distant shouts from the direction of the square and someone in uniform galloped by, but otherwise we could hear little but that incessant distant thunder of guns that had been going on for more than nine hours.

At last, quite suddenly, it ceased. Outside it was a still moonlit night.

'Is that the end?' said Carrie. 'We still don't know what's happened, but everything is over.'

CHAPTER FOURTEEN

We were not sure, even then, if the battle was truly over and we were still uncertain of the outcome. I sent a note down to my aunt and uncle saying that Carrie and I were staying in our room and would come down to see them before breakfast the next day. We then went back to bed still fully dressed and slept fitfully until awoken in the early hours of the morning by the sound of voices and heavy footfalls in the passage.

I went to the door and saw Henry Croft supporting his brother as they made their way, with some difficulty, to their room. Charles was scarcely recognisable. His uniform was plastered with half-dried yellow mud, his face blackened by gun smoke against which his eyes showed bloodshot and wild. He was bareheaded and his light-brown curls were as dirty as his face. His left hand was bound with a bloody rag and supported by a sling made from his sash.

'Elizabeth!' he croaked. 'It does me good to see you. I thought we'd never meet again. No, don't touch me, my dear, or I'll probably fall over.'

'I found him on the way back to Brussels,' said Sir Henry, 'limping along with a sergeant of his company. He insisted they should take it in turns to ride.'

'Well, Jack Green and I undertook to haul each other back to Brussels, so he deserved what help we could give,' said his brother hoarsely. 'I'm lucky – I only mislaid a couple of fingers and there's a contusion on my hip that makes me walk lame.'

'Hasn't a surgeon attended to you yet?' I enquired anxiously.

'That's the first funny thing I've heard today. They're fully occupied cutting off arms and legs – and heads too, for all I know. My poor fingers will have to wait.'

The cheerful tone was forced and behind it I could detect an infinite weariness.

'I'm damnably tired,' he said. 'None of us had much sleep the last few nights. During the action you don't notice, but now I could sleep like a log on a log. I've been up to my neck in mud, rye and a sandpit. Nothing like the army for variety.'

'What happened?' I asked. 'Have the French withdrawn? If the fighting continues tomorrow at least you'll be out of it.'

'You mean you don't know! Good God, no, I suppose you don't. The French have withdrawn all right – fled, finished.'

'Can it be true?'

'The general advance began at sunset. I got my fingers smashed in the late afternoon, but I hung on until I could see which way it was going. But when we started to move forward I decided to come back and get patched up.'

'The Duke isn't hurt?'

'No; it's a miracle for he was in the thick of it all day and nearly all his staff got hit.'

'Then all's well – this really is the end? The French are beaten?' Carrie's tremulous voice came over my shoulder.

'I suppose so. I can't see them coming back for a second helping. Even the Imperial Guard broke and fled at the last, or so I've heard. I found it difficult to see anything but clouds of smoke. It really was very bad, you know – worse than any of our battles in Spain. After them we used to ask who'd been killed. This time we asked who was still alive.'

'Did your friend Lieutenant Kincaid survive?' asked Carrie hesitantly.

'Yes, he's unhurt. Luck of the devil that one! He's stayed behind with his men – or what's left of them. You can rest safely in your beds for the rest of the night, my dears, and I'll go and adopt a horizontal posture in a state of blissful unconsciousness. Goodnight, ladies!'

'Come along, Charles, you need rest,' said Sir Henry, who was obviously eager to get his brother to bed.

When Carrie and I went back into our room we hugged each other in relief and delight.

'It's true! It's all over! We needn't feel frightened again.'

Certainly the fears had come to an end, but in some ways the worst was to follow.

On our way downstairs next morning Carrie and I felt more light-hearted than for many a day.

'All we need to know now', said Carrie, 'is that Ben is alive and well and then Papa and Mama will stop worrying.'

Her wish was granted sooner than we expected. On one of the landings we encountered an officer in a grimy red coat with a dirty face, bloodshot eyes and his arm in a sling.

'Why, it's Lieutenant Hayward!' I exclaimed, recognising Ben's fellow officer behind the mask of gun smoke, mud and blood.'

'Yes, I take it you've heard Boney's beat?'

'Sir Henry Croft brought his brother back in the middle of the night. They told us. We sent a message downstairs to my uncle and aunt.'

'I've just called on them to tell them their son, Ben Wakefield, is unhurt. He asked me to reassure his family.'

'Oh, how wonderful!' cried Carrie. 'They'll be so relieved'

I am ashamed to say I felt nothing save gratitude that my aunt and uncle had been spared the sorrow of a bereavement.

'And how is Ensign Parker?' continued Carrie cheerfully.

His expression changed. 'I'm afraid he's gone across the Styx. He was holding the colours, standing straight as a ramrod, and a cannonball took his head clean off. He couldn't have felt a thing. He was holding the staff so tight that the colour sergeant had to break his fingers to – I'm sorry, I'm too outspoken. You've both gone quite pale.'

'It's all right,' I said, 'we're not going to faint, but it's such a shock. Poor little Parker – only sixteen.' I thought of that fresh schoolboy face obliterated in an instant.

'Worse things happened. At least he didn't suffer, poor lad.'

'And you're hurt yourself.'

'A musket ball in the shoulder. Could be worse. I wondered if that Kean fellow could dig it out for me. He was a naval surgeon, wasn't he?'

'I'm sure he will. He's been treating the wounded for the last few days.'

'Then I'll go up to my room. I'm dead on my feet. If you see him, would you tell him?'

'Of course.'

He went on his way and Carrie and I continued downstairs to share the rejoicing with my uncle and aunt, though I was thinking of poor little Parker the last time I saw him, so proud of carrying the colours, whistling as he went on his way.

I left Carrie with her parents and went out on my own. I wished to see more of Brussels than I could glimpse from my hotel window. Almost immediately I encountered Mr Kean wearing a bloodstained apron. He told me that the wounded had been arriving all night and straw was being spread in the hotel courtyard.

I told him that Captain Croft and Lieutenant Hayward both needed attention, and he nodded briskly.

'I've already attended to Captain Croft. The poor lad fell asleep last night while his brother was pulling off his boots, so he left him in his dirt until this morning. Sir Henry and that manservant have managed to clean him up. I 'snipped off' a couple of fingers, as he put it, and applied a poultice to that nasty contusion. He thought there might be a splinter in there, but there wasn't. Then he drank half a tumbler of brandy and went back to sleep, which will do him more good than anything.

'I'll certainly attend to Lieutenant Hayward. It's the poor devils coming in that I'm concerned about. Thousands, I understand, and thousands more lying out on the battlefield.'

'I must help,' I said, 'and don't tell me to scrape lint. My father was a surgeon.'

'Was he, now?' Mr Kean smiled. 'And he taught you his trade? Amputations and all?'

'No, of course not. I was only six when he died. He taught me to bandage my dolls, that was all. But if you show me how to apply dressings I'm sure I could be of assistance.'

'I could certainly do with some help if you promise not to swoon at the sight of blood.'

'I've already seen a fair amount and I've not swooned yet.'

'Then come into the courtyard in about an hour and we'll see what you're capable of. If you start by dealing with minor injuries perhaps you can grow accustomed a little at a time. Go and get some fresh air. You're going to need it.'

He went charging off upstairs to find Lieutenant Hayward, and I went out into the street, which had already filled up with wounded. Under the archway leading to the courtyard I saw an empty wagon departing. I went to investigate and saw members of the hotel household raking straw over the cobbles under the direction of Monsieur Dubois, the proprietor, who was in his shirtsleeves with his red nightcap still on his head. There was a certain amount of swearing and shouting, but at last he was satisfied, just as a cartload of wounded was brought in. I kept out of the way and went on down the street in the direction of the Place Royale, which was rapidly filling up with the injured.

'A sad sight.' A voice spoke behind me. 'Brussels has changed from a fête to a charnel house.' Sir Henry Croft stood beside me and I was relieved to see him. 'Charles is asleep with Dobbs in attendance, so I just left them to it. That Kean knows what he's doing – very quick and competent. I offered him some of the brandy afterwards, but he declined so I've brought it out with me to offer these poor fellows.'

'And I've a bottle of water, so we can make a start. I asked Mr Kean if I could help him and he agreed providing I don't swoon.'

'I can't imagine you doing that, though I wonder if you have any real idea of what the work entails. You'll see some grim sights.'

'I've already seen some, taking food and water to the wounded from Quatre Bras.'

We took round our brandy and water until it was all gone and then I returned to the hotel courtyard, where Mr Kean was already at work. He advised me to collect an apron from the kitchen and then gave me my instructions.

'You can begin by washing their faces and giving them plenty to drink. They spent most of yesterday biting cartridges so they've practically eaten gunpowder. After that you can come round with me and observe the application of dressings. Then you can wash minor wounds and bandage them, or use adhesive plaster, whichever is appropriate. If there seems to be a serious injury or if you're unsure about something, then tell me. One of the maids is helping for as long as she can be spared from other duties. The pump is over there and if you feel nauseous, which is not unusual with beginners, there's a bucket provided.'

It seemed an interminable day. Indeed, at the time it seemed like the longest day of my life. I had never before been so exposed to the sufferings of others. What was hardest to bear was not the dirt, the blood, the hideous wounds, which drove me to the bucket by the pump several times, but the gentleness and gratitude of the men. They were invariably courteous, thanking me for the simplest assistance: a drink of water, a washed face, a bandaged ankle.

'Don't bother any more with me, Miss – there's others worse off.'

'I know this leg's got to come off, so don't trouble yourself with it. You've got enough to do.'

Once or twice Sir Henry came to see me. He had bought more brandy to take round the streets and then set off on his horse to Waterloo to assist some of the walking casualties.

In the middle of the afternoon he suggested I should take a rest.

'Don't work too hard, Elizabeth,' he said. 'If you wear yourself out and collapse you won't be able to continue. I've spoken to Kean and he's going to do one or two amputations on that kitchen table they've just brought out. I've undertaken to hold the leg, which I'm sure you wouldn't wish to attempt. Go and have something to eat and drink and rest for an hour. You'll be glad to know the chef and his assistants have returned to the kitchen, so I presume meals will resume their former regularity. Go now; I'll send for you when you are needed.'

I think he wanted to get me out of the way of the worst horrors, though what I had seen already was bad enough. I was almost relieved to take his advice.

As I could not face the climb to my bedroom I went up to the first landing and sat in the window embrasure, which had a padded seat. If I leaned back and drew up my feet I was reasonably comfortable. Below in the street I could see the rows of wounded on the pavement and a wagon disgorging yet more into the arms of the local citizens. There were a number of women, some no older than myself, giving assistance or handing out water. I think I dozed off for a while.

When I woke I did not feel at all hungry, but I was extremely thirsty. My uncle and aunt's room was close at hand and I thought they might provide me with a drink. As I entered, my aunt and Carrie both shrieked with horror and Uncle Nat at once took hold of me and made me sit down in an armchair.

'What a fright you look!' cried Carrie. 'You're covered in blood – it's even on your hands. Ugh! What have you been doing?'

'Isn't it obvious?' said my uncle impatiently.

The scene was one of comfortable domesticity, a thousand miles away from the horrors of the courtyard. They had just had a tray of tea brought in and I eagerly swallowed two cupfuls, which revived me considerably.

'You shouldn't be doing this; it's not right for a young girl,' said Aunt Hetty reprovingly.

'I'm twenty-three, not sixteen. Besides, others are helping, some of them my age. The poor men are so grateful, so brave and uncomplaining. They've given so much.'

'I'm sure it's a very fine thing you are doing,' said Uncle Nat, 'but young ladies are not meant to see such things.'

I was not far from tears, but I could not break down in case the three of them saw it as a sign of weakness and proof that I could not cope with the task I had set myself.

I did go back and gave assistance for as long as I could until a strong arm went round me to give me support, and a voice said, 'You have done enough now and you must rest. I'll have some supper sent up to you.'

It was Sir Henry, tired and dishevelled, his neckcloth spattered with blood.

'I'll stay a little longer and do what I can. Kean's half dead on his feet. Goodnight, my dear. You can come and see Charles tomorrow. I'm sure you'll do him good.'

I have no recollection of going up to my room, or of eating anything that had been provided. I only know I flung myself on the bed fully dressed and fell instantly asleep. Carrie joined me later, but I was quite unaware of her presence; and when I woke, some hours later, I found the room in darkness. When I took off the apron I found the blood had soaked through to my muslin dress. I pulled it off and dropped it on the floor, managed a perfunctory wash, dragged a comb through my tangled hair and fell back into bed to sleep until morning.

The morrow brought fresh horrors, but of a different sort.

CHAPTER FIFTEEN

Next morning on our way to breakfast we visited my uncle and aunt. Both seemed much more cheerful and told us delightedly that Ben had been to see them during the night.

'He had to get permission to leave the battlefield, but all is still in chaos there,' Aunt Hetty told us, scarcely able to contain her delight. 'He hadn't time to go up and see you girls and he was talking with your uncle on the landing for ages.'

'No more than ten minutes,' Uncle Nat interposed.

'Well, it seemed like ages to me. I don't know what it was about; I couldn't hear.'

'I expect he was telling Uncle things that might upset you,' I suggested.

'Probably, but I was so glad he was unhurt I wasn't greatly bothered about anything else. He looked a fright too. He said he'd cleaned himself up, but he was still filthy and smelt of gunpowder. I wish he'd never gone in the army. It's far too dangerous and they can't even keep clean.'

'They're all like that, Aunt,' I said, 'but it's finished now. He won't be in danger again; he'll be off to Paris with the Army of Occupation. I shouldn't think they'll encounter much resistance. Perhaps when you're well enough you'll be able to join him there.'

All the time this conversation was going on I was aware of a certain shiftiness in my uncle's demeanour. He looked happy enough; he smiled and nodded and made a few pertinent remarks and told me not to overexert myself, but there seemed to be an underlying unease. Something was going on of which I knew nothing, but I was sure it was connected with Ben's nocturnal visit.

I did not mention any of this to Sir Henry Croft, who stood up as I entered the dining room and indicated an empty chair beside him. I was rather relieved that Carrie had elected to stay with her parents for breakfast. I told him of Ben's visit, but said nothing of the uncertainty I felt.

'The army moved on to Nivelles yesterday afternoon,' he said, looking rather puzzled. 'Charles says Lord Wellington never keeps them lingering at a battlefield. Beside, they're in pursuit of the remains of the French Army. I suppose Ben had permission to come here briefly as long as he rejoined his regiment at Nivelles today. There's been a lot of coming and going and great confusion. I believe quite a few officers have come back to Brussels briefly to see their loved ones, but he left it rather late.'

'Knowing Ben, I wouldn't put too much faith in anything he told his parents.'

'Well, it's not your responsibility. Do you think you could come up and see Charles before you get involved in your medical work? He's longing to see you.'

I agreed willingly and found Charles sitting in an armchair by the open window, clad in a dressing gown over a clean white shirt. He was freshly washed and shaved, his appearance slightly gaunt but almost back to normal.

'Ah!' he cried. 'A sight for sore eyes!'

He flung the book he was reading on the bed, took his bandaged hand out of its sling, and held out his arms to me. I could do no more than go into them and accept his embrace.

'I wanted to reclaim that kiss,' he whispered.

I kissed him lightly on the cheek. 'There you have it,' I said.

'Is that all?'

'I'm afraid so.'

'It's Henry, isn't it? I should have known.'

'What's this about me?' Sir Henry, who had been standing with his back to the door, came forward to join us.

'I feel so much better,' said Charles, pretending not to hear him. 'I think I might manage to go out tomorrow for a little while. It's confounded dull staying in here with nothing to see below but lines of wounded.'

'We'll see about that,' said his brother. 'You've been told to rest.'

'It's only my hand and the leg is much better. In the meantime, Elizabeth, have you got anything amusing for me to read? Henry here has some very worthy books, but all too serious for me in my present state. I need something cheerful that doesn't need great concentration.'

'I've *Castle Rackrent* in my room,' I said. 'Have you read it?'

'One of Miss Edgeworth's, I believe? No, I haven't.'

'Then I'll fetch it for you,' I offered. 'It's quite amusing.'

On the way back, clutching the novel, I saw Lieutenant Hayward coming towards me down the passage, looking rather pale and sickly, but a good deal cleaner than the last time we had met. His arm was still in a sling.

I wished him good morning, adding the hope that he was feeling better.

'Not much, but I can't stand being there on my own any longer. Kean tried to locate the musket ball. He poked around with his fingers and then tried a probe and forceps, but said it was in too deep and I'd have to live with it. Of course, they do work their way out sometimes, so I'll have to hope that happens. At least it isn't anywhere vital and nothing's broken. I think of poor little Parker and feel lucky.'

'My cousin Ben called to see his parents last night,' I said. 'He didn't come up to see his sister and me, so don't think he neglected you. I daresay he was keen to get back.'

'He'll have to make haste, but if he has the use of a horse he'll get there quickly enough to chase Boney all the way home.'

'My aunt and uncle were delighted to see him, of course, but I don't think he told them much about the battle.'

'He acquitted himself well for a Johnny Newcome, but I don't think he enjoyed it as much as he thought he would.'

'That doesn't surprise me,' I said, 'but I've no doubt he'll pose as a great hero for the rest of his life.'

'He's welcome to it. I always preferred Parker.' He gave a

sardonic grin and went on his way downstairs.

Having left *Castle Rackrent* with Charles and ascertained that Sir Henry was riding out again to see what assistance he could give to the returning wounded, I made my way down to the courtyard. There had been some improvements since the previous day. Kean had had makeshift canvas awnings erected to protect his patients from the elements, and mattresses, sheets and pillows had appeared from several different sources. Madame Dubois herself had come out to help wash the men and put them into clean shirts.

In the corner next to the backstairs of the hotel lay one of my favourite patients, a cheerful Irishman whom everybody called Paddy, though I do not think that was his name. Next to Paddy was a space, once occupied by a corporal of the 52nd who had been sent back to his billets the previous afternoon.

'I'm going home today!' announced Paddy with delight.

'Home? Not back to County Cork, surely?'

'No, more's the pity, but back to my billets, where I'll have a proper bed and the mistress of the house fussing over me. I'll soon be meself again. 'Twas only a flesh wound, after all.'

'But a very nasty one. You lost a lot of blood.'

'I'll soon make some more with all the good food we've been getting in Brussels.' His expression changed and be beckoned me closer and spoke in a low voice. 'Something peculiar's been going on here, Miss. You see this space next to the steps.'

'Yes – Corporal Collins was there.'

'So he was, but last night somebody else took his place.'

'I don't understand.'

'Somebody', he whispered, 'brought a dead body down those back stairs and down the steps and laid it next to me. Dead but not stiff. *Recently* dead, you understand.'

'But who?'

'I don't know, but the uniform was that of an officer and he had a bandage round his throat as though he had a wound there. Of course, he may have been one of those officers from upstairs who died in the night, but why bring him down here? He was carried off in the death cart at dawn, so I suppose he'll be buried with other ranks. Strange business, eh?'

'Very strange.'

'And it gets stranger. The chaps who collected him had lanterns – it was still quite dusky, you know – and the officer's cap fell off as they picked him up. He'd a mop of hair like a fiery bonfire, he had! Not many like that.'

I turned cold. Ben had visited his parents in the night and his outstanding characteristic was his bright red-gold hair.

'But who was responsible for his death?' I asked Paddy.

'He wasn't killed in battle, I'm sure of that. I think he died in the night. If you ask me, I think it was the croakers.'

His voice sank even lower as he spoke the last words. It made no sense, but that is what it sounded like. There was an outburst of shouting as a fresh wagonload of wounded was brought in to fill the gaps left by the dead and recovering.

At that moment Mr Kean came over to me, rolling up his sleeves. For a few seconds I was distracted; I felt there was something I had missed.

'I never thanked you yesterday for all your hard work,' he said. 'Not many young women could do what you did. I thought you'd give up after an hour or two, but you stuck it out and now you're back for more. We had two more deaths in the night: that fair boy—'

'Oh no!'

'I wasn't surprised. These young fellows never do as well as the hardened men. The other was one of the amputations – the private, not the sergeant. We've got plenty more just arrived, so we'll make a start if you're ready.'

I had no further chance to speak to Paddy. He was taken away soon afterwards to make room for a newcomer and I did not know where his billets were. The day's work gave me little time to wonder about the mysterious red-headed corpse. I would, I felt sure, be able to find out if Ben had returned safely to his regiment.

In the afternoon a high-ranking member of the medical staff called to inspect the provision for the care of the wounded and pronounced himself well satisfied.

'You've got a regular little hospital here and the fresh air will help limit contagion. They couldn't get better treatment anywhere,' I heard him say, 'but, of course, you naval surgeons are second to none. At least you're not on a moving deck this time. Only one thing: that young lady looks worn out. Give her an afternoon off or you'll be a helper short. I'll send an orderly to assist you. We can ill spare one, but that's better than the young lady collapsing with exhaustion.'

They went on to discuss gangrene and I moved out of hearing.

Sir Henry Croft arrived soon after the visiting surgeon departed and suggested I should rest for an hour while more amputations were carried out. I agreed wearily and this time decided to climb up those endless steps to my room, where I could stretch out on my bed. Sir Henry had promised to send up a chambermaid with tea and toast, though I had little appetite for anything but liquids.

As I ascended the stairs I heard masculine voices conversing ahead of me. I could not see the speakers owing to the bend in the stairs, but they stopped talking suddenly. They must have heard my footsteps.

I found two strange newcomers sitting in one of the window embrasures, obviously resting on their way to the rooms above. Some of these rooms had been vacated by their previous occupants in the panic that preceded the battle. Others had been used by officers who had been killed or were moving on with the army to the French border. Some injured officers had been accommodated in the hotel, but on the lower floors. Up above there were still vacant bedrooms.

One of the strangers was a small individual with a large bald head and an ingratiating smile.

'Amos Bowles.' He introduced himself, rising and bowing a little too obsequiously.

His companion said nothing. He was taller than Bowles, but still rather small and wore a German greatcoat – Prussian perhaps – and a dirty, soft-topped peaked cap pulled low over his eyes. His face was blackened by gun smoke and swathed in bandages.

I would not normally have spoken to strange men in a hotel, but the times were so out of joint that when they offered me a salutation I replied by informing them that medical attention was available in the courtyard.

'You look, sir, as though you have been wounded quite badly,' I said, directing my observation to the German, if that's what he was.

'*Ja,*' he replied in a guttural tone, '*danke schön.*'

That was the limit of my German and I suspected it was the limit of his. He seemed to have understood me, but was unwilling to venture speaking English. Amos Bowles was a Londoner, from the little I heard him say, but I continued on my way without giving them much thought. Brussels was full of strange people of every nationality.

It was only later, when drinking my tea, that I realised the two men had been speaking in English before they saw me. I could not hear the actual words, but the language was unmistakeable.

The next day the German – except I felt sure he was not German at all – stood aside on the stairs to let me pass. I looked at him more closely this time. Why was he wearing a heavy grey coat on such a hot day, with the collar turned up too? He still had not washed his face, and the little I could see was smoothly black. I had seen enough of the dirt of battle to recognise the mixture of smoke, sweat, mud and blood that masked so many features and, with the lower ranks, the incrustations of gunpowder from cartridge-biting. This was more like the result of holding a saucer over a candle.

'*Guten Morgen,*' I said cheerfully.

'*Ja,*' he muttered, and hurried on his way.

'A disguise,' I thought, 'and not a very good one. I think I know who you are, *mein Herr.*'

He and his travelling companion never seemed to be together, but I saw Bowles a little later in the entrance hall of the hotel, about to go out of the front door. He had an enormous leather satchel over his shoulder and I could not help wondering what it was intended to contain.

'Please forgive me for interrupting your work,' I said, trying to surmise what that work might be, 'but I would like to ask you something.'

At once he seemed wary, his eyes swivelling to see if anyone was in earshot.

'It doesn't concern you, but your travelling companion.'

He at once relaxed and even smiled in an unpleasantly servile way.

'How can I be of assistance?'

'I wondered how you met the German gentleman. Do you know him well?'

He shrugged. 'We met in Ghent. I was on my way from Ostend. My employer sent me over from London. That fellow – Herr Schmidt he calls himself – introduced himself at an inn and suggested we should travel together and share expenses. Our accommodation would be cheaper if there were two of us. I agreed. I could tell right away he wasn't German. He comes from London, same as me, and told some cock-and-bull yarn about being on a secret mission with the Prussians. A likely story! I wondered if he was a deserter, but, if so, why did he want to come back to Brussels? None of my business! I didn't say much, but as I was saving money I didn't complain.'

I eyed him doubtfully. Why had his employer sent him to Brussels? And what was the purpose of that great satchel? I let him go.

It was a week or two before I found out why he was here.

CHAPTER SIXTEEN

A great silence and paralysis seemed to have fallen on the city of Brussels. All gaiety and recreation had vanished; uniforms were still to be seen about the streets, but their wearers were pale and haggard and moved no more with their old brisk gait. They hobbled on crutches or walked slowly along with arm in a sling or head bandaged. Through windows open to the warm summer air could be glimpsed heads resting on pillows or leaning against the backs of chairs. Every door bore a chalked inscription: *'Trois militaires blessés . . . Quatre officiers blessés'*. Funerals were a common sight and many wounded still lay in the streets.

My free afternoon was to be spent, in part, with the Croft brothers as Charles had declared himself well enough to walk in the park. I was rather annoyed when Carrie obtained her parents' permission to go with us as I had hoped to have Henry and Charles to myself. This was not entirely selfish as I wanted to tell them Paddy's strange story and I did not want to upset Carrie by suggesting her brother might have met a violent death off the battlefield. She was not particularly devoted to Ben, but he *was* her brother and sometimes showed a shallow, vaguely fraternal affection.

'I would have died of suffocation if I'd stayed indoors any longer,' she declared. 'I'm sick of scraping lint and looking out of the window at injured men.'

'You'll see plenty more out here,' Sir Henry warned her. 'The whole city has become a giant hospital.'

Even Charles seemed rather subdued, especially when he heard from a passing acquaintance that the Duke of Wellington had joined the army at Nivelles yesterday and was due to cross the French border today.

'I wish I was with them,' he said gloomily.

He seemed glad to sit down on a bench in the park and I thought that the walk from the hotel, although short, had tired him more than he would admit.

The once cheerful park, with its crowds of military gallants and pretty women, had become a dreary place. Men in shabby uniforms limped by, leaning on sticks or supported by friends.

I tried to distract Charles by asking him the meaning of 'croakers'. I was eager to find out more about Paddy's curious remarks without giving too much away in front of Carrie.

'I don't mean frogs,' I said. 'I mean how would a soldier use the word?'

'Why, croakers are people who do nothing but whine and complain.'

'That's what I thought it meant.'

This was not very satisfactory, and I was about to question him further when my attention was entirely diverted by the sight of two people I knew walking along the path towards us.

'Why,' cried Carrie, 'it's Lady Silbury's daughter Lydia and that governess/companion! Ben's rather sweet on her, you know – Lydia, not the companion.'

'Yes,' said Charles, 'we all noticed that at the picnic.'

'The Silburys all went to Antwerp, didn't they, with that odious Moffat's wife?' said Carrie.

The men stood up, but after nodding an acknowledgment Lydia kept her distance and beckoned to me. She indicated we should sit on a bench across the path from the others.

'Forgive me for approaching you in this way, Miss Aston,' she said. 'I did wonder whether to call at your hotel, so I am pleased to see you now. We started from Antwerp at dawn, so Mama is quite exhausted and lying down in her room. I needed a breath of air after being in a carriage for so long, especially in the company of that Moffat woman.'

'She has come back with you?'

'Of course. We dropped her off at your hotel. She was sure

her husband would be waiting for her.

'I think not. He tried to escape to Ostend, taking my cousin Carrie with him. She soon found out her mistake, but fortunately Mr Fox went after them and brought her back.'

'Did you know Fox was employed by my mother?'

'He's never mentioned her name, but I gathered that was so.'

'She's a little afraid of Moffat – I don't really know why. She won't confide in me; she thinks I'm a silly young girl. I think it's something to do with my father's will. I imagine she signed, or agreed to something illegal, which she'd been tricked into by Moffat. It's possible he has some documents which would prove her guilt. She employed Fox to get them back, but so far he hasn't been successful. He *did* recover some jewellery Moffat had taken from her.'

'Ah yes, Moffat said it was his wife's and had been stolen. I didn't believe him.'

'The man's a complete rogue. Where did he go, do you suppose?'

I shrugged. I had my own ideas, but as yet could prove nothing.

'We thought you'd come back yesterday,' I said. 'Many people did.'

'Oh yes! People in Antwerp were running around in their nightclothes cheering and shouting, but there had been so many dreadful rumours: that the Duke had been fatally wounded and our army routed. Mama would not return until she was absolutely sure that all was well.'

'If you can call it *well*,' I said, nodding at a young officer on crutches who went by at that moment with an anxious female in attendance.

'Captain Croft is wounded,' she said. 'I can see his hand is in bandages.'

'He had two fingers amputated and he's got a nasty contusion which makes him walk lame.'

'I'm sorry, but it could have been so much worse. The real reason I wanted to see you concerns your cousin Lieutenant Wakefield. Do you know if he is with the army? We heard they are about to invade France.'

'So I believe. They moved away from the battlefield the following day.'

'I found a package had been left for me at the Hôtel Belle Vue, so I presume Ben must have come back to Brussels for a while.'

'He came to see his parents on the evening of the 19th. Obviously he called at your hotel the same evening. Carrie and I didn't see him – I suppose he was in a hurry to rejoin his regiment.'

She produced a small bundle that scarcely filled her hand. It was a tightly rolled man's handkerchief tied bound with a crimson silk thread that looked as though it had been pulled from an officer's sash. Tucked into the thread was a scrap of paper addressed to 'The Hon. Lydia Silbury, Hôtel Belle Vue'. She unwrapped the package to reveal something folded inside – a note, which she handed to me to read.

19 June, Field of Battle

My dearest –
    Please accept the enclosed as a token of my love. I shall have it made into a ring when we are able to announce our engagement.
I am unhurt.
    Your devoted B. W.

Then Lydia showed me the item Ben had enclosed. It looked like a segment broken from a necklace or tiara. It blazed with diamonds of the finest quality, including one that was surely between four and five carats. I was not a jeweller's niece for nothing.

'This is very valuable,' I observed. 'Where do you suppose he obtained it?'

'I have no idea. Do you think there will be any more battles?'

'Captain Croft thinks not. He says Bonaparte's army was quite broken and in disarray, but there may be some small resistance from one or two fortresses on the way to Paris.'

'I hope that's true. I've been so anxious and that horrid Moffat woman did nothing but quote the Bible at us – all the most dismal predictions she could remember.'

'She'll have a great shock when she discovers her beloved husband tried to decamp to Ostend with a seventeen-year-old girl.'

Lydia came over to exchange a few words with Carrie and the Croft brothers.

111

'I will always treasure memories of that picnic,' she said. 'It was such a happy day.'

'Especially', added Charles, 'when one thinks of those who will never return: poor little Parker, for instance.'

'He's dead?' She looked genuinely shocked. 'Oh, I'm so sorry; he was such a nice boy, so full of fun. I'll be glad to get away from here – it's so dismal now.'

She turned back to her silent companion, murmuring that she must get back to her mama at the Hôtel Belle Vue, and so left us.

Charles seemed thoroughly dispirited. 'I was thinking of that picnic,' he said. 'Life will never be quite the same again. I've had enough. Let's go back to the hotel.'

When we reached our destination I was surprised to see Mr Fox lounging about smoking outside the door. I stopped to talk to him, and my companions, giving me a rather odd look, went on their way upstairs without me.

'Can we go inside?' I suggested. 'There's a bench where we can sit. I've something important to tell you. At least, I *think* it's important.'

He at once knocked out his pipe and conducted me indoors, where we sat on a bench in an alcove. I told him very briefly the strange story related by Paddy and the curious event this afternoon when the Honourable Lydia had shown me her diamonds.

'My dear young lady!' he exclaimed. You are quite right to tell me. There is indeed something strange going on, and I promise to investigate the moment the present situation is resolved. I have a duty to my employer.'

'Lady Silbury? I know. Her daughter told me about it this afternoon.'

'Ah, then I can trust you to keep a confidence. Matters are about to come to a head. Mrs Moffat has returned.'

'Yes, but her husband has disappeared. How do you know he didn't go on to Ostend? Perhaps he's in England by now.' I did not quite believe what I was saying, but I wanted to hear what Fox had to say before divulging my own suspicions.

'I don't think so,' he smiled. 'Consider this: he got away from us with nothing but the clothes he stood up in. His valise was still in the gig. He probably had a little money and the papers he always carried with him to threaten poor Lady Silbury. If he went home to England, what awaited him there? A changed name, avoidance of family and friends, disgrace and penury. No, he needs his rich wife. He has to convince her all is well. I'm sure he can find some tall story to tell her. Someone who was a disciple of Joanna Southcott is used to swallowing fiction. As soon as he's convinced her, away they go to England.'

'He's still here, isn't he?'

'Oh yes, I saw him go in – heavily disguised, of course.'

'The German!' I cried. 'I knew there was something bogus about him, wearing a heavy greatcoat in this hot weather, and the dirt on his face didn't look genuine. As for those bandages . . .'

'Exactly! And he knows no more of the language than I do. He joined up with that Bowles to look less suspicious. There's another sly character! I wonder what he's up to with that great satchel? Never mind – let me sort out Moffat first. Would you like to come up with me? I'm sure he's not dangerous; in fact he's a pathetic little coward, otherwise I wouldn't suggest your presence. Your testimony may help convince that foolish wife of his.'

'You mean he's up there with her now?'

'Oh yes, I saw him go in. He didn't see me – I took care of that.'

'But if he's not dangerous, what about that poor dead woman in the park? Wasn't he responsible?'

'Ah, that's another story which need not concern us at present. All I want from him is that packet of documents.'

'Will he hand them over?'

'I think so. If not you can run for Sir Henry and his brother – they'll soon frighten him. Now, I'll lead the way, and if they've locked the door I've the means to unlock it.'

I followed Mr Fox up the hundred steps to our landing. I was half looking forward to the discomfiture of the Moffat couple and half afraid there might be some nasty surprise lying in wait for us.

CHAPTER SEVENTEEN

The door was not locked and, after telling me to stay in the passage and observe what was happening, Mr Fox tapped on the panels. The two voices inside fell silent suddenly and, without waiting for permission to enter, Fox flung open the door and stepped into the room.

'Ah, as I thought!' he exclaimed. 'Mr and Mrs Moffat reunited!'

Mrs Moffat looked much as usual, but a deep crimson hue crept up from her neck to her face.

Her husband was still in his Prussian coat, but had taken off his cap. Above his eyebrows his forehead was quite clean, but below he still bore the false hue of a battle he had never been near. The bandages had been pulled from his head and lay round his neck like an untidy muffler.

'What is the meaning of this impertinent behaviour?' cried Mrs Moffat indignantly. 'Bursting into a private room without so much as a by-your-leave!'

'Get out, sir!' shouted Mr Moffat, looking decidedly shaken. 'Get out at once or I – or I . . .'

'Or you'll what? Send for the law? I don't think the Belgian authorities will be very interested at present; and as far as your activities are concerned, *I* am the law! The time has come for you to hand over the documents which belong to my employer.'

'I don't know what you are talking about.'

'Oh yes you do! Now, madam, what has he been telling you about his activities since you parted?'

'My husband has been engaged on a secret mission for the Duke of Wellington.'

'I'm sure the Duke would be very surprised to hear it.'

'You've only to see the state my husband is in. He is still bearing the marks of battle. It's a wonder he wasn't killed in the service of his country. He was reporting on the progress of the Prussians so that the Duke would know when they were likely to arrive.'

'And you really believe that nonsense?' said Fox. 'Madam, I'm afraid I must disillusion you. While you were off to Antwerp with Lady Silbury your husband was abducting a young lady and taking her to Ostend. I caught them at Ghent and brought her safely back. If I had not managed to intercept them – on which occasion the heroic Mr Moffat ran off – he would undoubtedly have made an attempt to seduce the unfortunate girl. Would you like me to call her as a witness?'

'This is all preposterous,' Mr Moffat blustered. 'I was miles away. I don't know what this man is talking about. You do believe me, don't you, Phoebe?'

But Phoebe, for the first time, hesitated. 'What young lady are you referring to? Is it Miss Aston out there?'

'No,' I answered, stepping into the room, 'it was my cousin Carrie. She was so terrified that she believed your husband when he promised to take her to safety. She found out her mistake on the journey. He has told you a pack of fantastic lies.'

'Walter, what have you to say about this? Are they lying or are you? Have I nourished a viper in my bosom?'

At that moment Carrie came out of our room next door after hearing raised voices and some sort of commotion.

'That dreadful man!' she cried. 'I never thought I'd have the misfortune to see him again. How dare you come back, sir! I presume you're attempting to deny everything. Why are you dressed in that ridiculous fashion with your face covered in lampblack? There are plenty of real soldiers here who could prove you a liar in a very short time.'

'Walter!' exclaimed Mrs Moffat. 'I shall pack up again and depart. I am going back to London and don't you *dare* attempt to follow me. I never want to see you again. Get out of this room immediately.'

Mr Moffat appeared a broken man. Meekly he walked to the door, but was stopped by Mr Fox, who held out his hand. Moffat sighed and brought out a packet of papers from inside his coat.

'I'd like to see you brought to justice, but my employer will be quite satisfied with these. I trust they are all here.'

'Yes – yes! I'm sick to death of the whole business.'

'It's not quite over yet,' said Fox. 'You're coming with me to hand over these papers in person. I want the lady in question to check them carefully to make sure nothing is missing. Then you can beg her forgiveness. After that I don't care what you do.'

'But don't come back here,' commanded Mrs Moffat. 'I shall be gone! I have been mistaken in my assessment of character, but at least I still have control over my own money. My brother insisted that a proper marriage settlement should be drawn up before my marriage.'

'Very sensible,' said Mr Fox, 'but you may find you have not been married at all. Your so-called husband had a wife in the West Country when he went through a form of marriage with you.'

The high colour drained from her face and she sat down suddenly as though she had lost the use of her legs. I went to her with my smelling salts, but she waved me away.

'It does make matters simpler,' said Fox. 'Even if the first wife had subsequently died you are still not legally married. So he has no right to impose on you ever again.'

As Moffat followed Mr Fox through the door, Carrie shrieked and ran back into our room. Afterwards she told me how much she had enjoyed her abductor's downfall.

It occurred to me that had Fox and I not broken in upon the Moffats when we did the chances were that Mrs Moffat would have been persuaded to believe her spouse's fantastic story and would have decamped with him to Ostend. Anyone who had been a disciple of Joanna Southcott must be gullible indeed.

As it was he slunk away into oblivion and she was left to lament the shattering of her dreams. She was thoroughly disillusioned and I wondered, briefly, if it would have been better if her husband had not been unmasked in front of her. I suppose she would have found out sooner or later, but her experience of married bliss had been all too brief.

Later that day Fox came to tell me what had transpired at the Hôtel Belle Vue. Lady Silbury had checked through the incriminating documents while the guilty Moffat stood at a distance with a bowed head, twisting his cap in his hands. He then made a cringing admission of guilt and begged forgiveness.

Lady Silbury told him sharply not to talk nonsense – she was sure he wasn't really sorry at all, but only vexed because his plans had gone awry. Then she dismissed him from her presence.

'So that's the whole problem cleared up,' said Mr Fox with a certain degree of satisfaction.

'Yes, you must be very pleased. But one thing I don't understand. Why did it take you so long to confront the rogue?'

'I wanted to disgrace him in front of his wife so that he'd never trouble her or anyone else again. If I'd tackled him earlier he'd have wriggled out of it with her full support. The evidence of you and Miss Wakefield helped to convince her of his guilt.'

'Yes, I see that,' I said, but I did wonder if Mr Fox was not enjoying a pleasant, well-paid holiday in a foreign city, far from the sordid duties of Bow Street. It was, after all, in his interest to prolong his investigations, even if he had run the risk of losing the miscreant in Ghent. I believed the Bow Street officers were very well paid, especially when working privately, and I was soon to find out this was only too true.

'What about that poor woman in the park?' I asked. 'Was she his first wife? If not, who was she and who killed her?'

'Ah now, that would be telling. I'm not ready yet to reveal what I know. You must be patient, my dear young lady. Lady Silbury is perfectly satisfied and has paid me off, so I really have nothing to keep me here.'

I took this as a hint. 'I hope you won't go yet,' I said, 'because I wondered if you could undertake another investigation on my behalf. I don't know what you charge, but I'm sure I could afford to pay you. This would be very confidential as I don't want the rest of my family to know anything about it at present. It may prove to be too painful or it may be nothing at all.'

'And this concerns your cousin Lieutenant Wakefield and the curious story told by one of your patients. I said I thought it worth an inquiry, but you haven't yet told me all the details. I promise I'll keep it to myself. Discretion's my middle name.'

I told him all I knew and he seemed very interested.

'I'd like you to trace my cousin Ben,' I said. 'I want to know if he's rejoined his regiment or if he's disappeared – and if so, what's happened to him.'

'The army's moved on,' said Fox thoughtfully, 'and that presents a problem, but not an insuperable one.'

'Paddy's story was so odd. I'm sure he didn't dream it or make it up.'

'No, I shouldn't think he did. The red hair is a help. I'll let you know as soon as I find anything out. I'll begin by trying to find your friend Paddy, which should be easy enough as you know his regiment.'

'Then what will I owe you?'

'One guinea a day plus fourteen shillings for expenses. I hope that isn't too steep, Miss Aston.'

'I shall pay you for a fortnight's work. If you haven't completed the investigation by then we'll bring it to an end.'

'That sounds fair enough to me. Shall we shake hands on it?'

We sealed our bargain and he departed. I felt I could do no more for the time being. I owed little enough to my cousin Ben, but for the sake of his parents the truth had to be uncovered.

CHAPTER EIGHTEEN

The next day I returned to my work in the courtyard. I am not at all sure my afternoon of recreation had done me any good. Indeed, I found it more of a strain than before. Although I had become inured to the blood and smells, apart from the stench of gangrene, the burden of misery seemed heavier. I wrote letters to distant wives and mothers, wondering if they would reach their destination before the sender died. I tried to cheer those who seemed sunk in melancholy and leaned close to hear whispered last messages to those at home. It was this that wore me down, not the washing and bandaging.

And still they came in, four days after the battle, weak and helpless with scarcely any life left in them. There were more deaths than before.

On the Friday morning I saw Fox standing at the door above the steps, beckoning to me. I went over, wiping my hands on my apron.

'Some bad news, I'm afraid, Miss Aston. I managed to trace your informant, Michael Doyle, known to one and all as Paddy. He suffered a great haemorrhage and died.'

'No!' I was aghast.

'His landlady's in floods of tears. She'd made rather a pet of him. So there's no chance now of him adding to the story. The best we can do is find the men who gathered up the corpses that morning. They may have some recollection of a red-haired officer and be able to tell us where he is buried. I'll also see about contacting his regiment. If we find he's alive and well, then there's nothing to investigate. I'll be off, then. Sorry to be the bearer of bad tidings.'

He went, leaving me at the top of the steps. I looked down at the courtyard with Mr Kean busy probing, lancing and stitching. He seemed tireless. One of his patients told me that he even came down in the night to check the condition of the wounded in his care.

A chambermaid was going round with a basin, washing faces and minor wounds and chatting cheerfully in her limited English. I would not be needed for a little while.

A tide of grief rose to overwhelm me and I could endure my surroundings no more. I toiled up to my room, my legs almost too heavy to bear me. Why did I suddenly feel old at twenty-three? I reached the door, fumbled with the key and, beginning to weep, managed to turn it in the lock. Leaving the door wide open I ran in and flung myself on the bed in a storm of tears. I do not think I had ever experienced such wrenching sobs. They came as a relief, but they did not stop.

I was aware that someone had come into the room and was sitting on the bed beside me. I was lifted from the pillow and enfolded in strong arms which held me very close.

'My poor girl,' a voice murmured in my ear. 'This was bound to happen. You were never meant to endure such horrors.' Sir Henry Croft produced a handkerchief and helped me to mop my wet eyes and cheeks. 'You must be exhausted,' he said.

Still he held me close and I pressed my face into his shoulder, striving to master myself.

'It's not the work,' I whispered. 'It's not even the blood and the wounds and feeling tired all the time. It's the pathos – the deaths. There were three this morning. One fell aside as I touched his shoulder. Another asked me to hold his hand. The third was the worst – he thought I was his mother. It's becoming unbearable.'

I calmed a little at last, finding relief in talking to Sir Henry, who had always seemed patient and sympathetic. Then I became aware of my situation: half lying on my bed in the embrace of a man I had always found attractive. He began to kiss me, holding me so tightly I could hardly breathe. He pulled off the scarf with which I had covered my head, loosened the pins and thrust his fingers into my hair.

'My dear girl, you must know how much I love and admire you!'

His kisses grew more urgent and I found myself instinctively responding. I had long returned his love and admiration, but had been unable to speak of it until now. I told him what I felt.

Suddenly he broke away.

'No, this won't do! Forgive me! This is entirely my fault and it won't happen again. I've allowed my feelings to run away with me. I should never have let it occur – it can lead to nothing. Marriage is out of the question and I respect you far too much to hope for anything else. Forgive me!' He almost ran from the room.

'Marriage is out of the question.' But why? Was it something to do with the fact that I was far beneath him socially? A surgeon's daughter is lowly indeed compared with a member of the landed gentry, even one as impoverished as Sir Henry Croft. I had not thought he was a snob, but such notions run deep.

Surely he was not married already? He had never mentioned a wife, but that did not mean she did not exist.

I could think of nothing else that could keep us apart, a mutual love having been declared.

My own disappointments seemed trivial compared with what I had been witnessing every day, but I still felt bitter regret and bafflement.

I wept again for the three young men who had died that day and for Ensign Parker and poor dear Paddy, who would never see County Cork again. But now, succumbing to self-pity, I also wept for myself.

Later that day, when the chance arose to speak to Charles Croft on his own, I broached the subject rather bluntly, but could see no subtle way to do it.

'Charles, this may seem a strange question, but has your brother ever been married?'

'Good God no! At least – unless he formed a mésalliance while I was away in the Peninsula. He doesn't tell me everything, you know. He thinks too much. Such men are dangerous, or so

Shakespeare says. I don't know if it's true or not. What made you ask?'

'Oh, nothing really – just a rather odd remark he made.'

'Take no notice, he's always making odd remarks. I don't know about thinking, but he certainly reads too much and that gives him strange ideas sometimes. You are very fond of him, aren't you?'

I nodded, not trusting myself to speak.

'Don't let yourself love him too much. You may be hurt.' There was a pause and he squeezed my hand. Then he continued, more cheerfully. 'Now, if you'd chosen me it would have been a very different story. We'd have had a high old time in Paris with the Army of Occupation; but after that, half-pay for the rest of my life, I suppose, unless I joined some regiment in India or somewhere equally insalubrious. But it wouldn't be the same after all those years of adventure. I wouldn't care to serve under any other commander-in-chief. After you've fought for Caesar it's not the same with Sir Huffington-Puffington. I suppose I could find some occupation in civil life: inspector of prisons, customs and excise officer or some such. Not an agreeable prospect to think the best part of your life is over at twenty-six. On the other hand, I wouldn't care to go through another heap of glory like this last.' He looked glum.

'I'm sure you'll always make your way in life, Charles, if only because you cheer everybody up.'

'Do I?' He sounded genuinely surprised.

'Bless you, Charles. I hope we may always be friends.'

'I'm sure we will be, but try not to hope for anything more from Henry. I don't think he'll ever marry. Now don't look so miserable. Life is very difficult for you at present, but it won't last. I'll go to Paris and you'll go home.'

'And your brother?'

He shrugged. 'He may stay here. I don't think he's decided yet.'

A couple of days later Fox came to tell me that he'd found the men responsible for collecting the dead from two of the hospitals and the Hôtel Britannique. They told him where they were buried, in a mass grave, and a Protestant minister conducted the service.

'If you want an exhumation his parents will have to be involved.'

'No, I don't want them to be told. Not yet, anyway.'

'I found a courier leaving with dispatches for the army heading for Paris. He agreed to deliver a letter to your cousin's commanding officer, so we should know, in a week or two, whether he's now with his regiment. I take it you haven't heard from him?'

'No, but that's not unusual. My cousin Ben is a very bad correspondent. I pray he's still alive. I don't want my aunt and uncle hurt. Death in battle is one thing; this is something criminal.'

Fox shrugged. 'My life's been spent dealing with "something criminal". This is an interesting case and unlike anything I've dealt with before.'

'This situation is different from anything we have ever known,' I said.

I returned to my work in the courtyard. I told myself it would not go on forever and I tried to steel myself against the most painful experiences.

Kean asked me if I felt able to go on and looked concerned. 'I'd be sorry to lose you,' he said, 'especially as we're not going to get any fresh casualties now, so the end is in sight. I don't know what I'd have done without you. But you've already excelled yourself. I'd quite understand if you felt you'd done enough.'

'No,' I said, 'I feel better now. I'll continue for as long as I'm needed.'

to warn her of the horrors ahead. Sir Henry had advised us to wear stout shoes and to take smelling salts and eau de cologne to ward off the foul smells, but Carrie appeared in dainty kid slippers. I had always thought she had no imagination.

The Crofts had hired a carriage as Sir Henry refused to allow his brother to ride. The other occupants were Uncle Nat and Mr Kean, who had been invited to join the party as he was anxious to see the scene of the engagement. All the men were armed, or so I was informed.

It was a bright, warm day, the sunlight flickering through the beeches of the Forêt de Soignes, but a desolate and evil atmosphere hung over the road. The *chausée* itself was deeply rutted, so we were severely jolted, but it was the smells and sights on either side of us that cast a gloom over the party. Even Carrie stopped chattering and held her open fan to shield her from her squalid surroundings.

Everywhere lay the wreckage of an army: overturned carts, shattered wheels, scraps of harnesses and bits of uniforms; shoes, caps, rags, papers, heaps of soggy biscuit and empty knapsacks, with here and there the bloated carcass of an unburied horse. Between the trees, in muddy hollows, lay ominous pools of reddish water and shallow mounds of freshly turned earth marked the burial places of the wounded who had died on the way to Brussels. The air was thick with the stink of corruption, so that the carriage horses whinnied in fright and we brought out smelling salts and vinaigrettes.

Lady Silbury produced a bottle of eau de cologne and splashed the scent liberally around the carriage, but it made little difference.

We were forced to travel slowly owing to the state of the road until at last we reached the village of Waterloo. On cottage doors were still chalked the names of high-ranking officers who had lodged there the night before the battle and were now dead or fearsomely injured.

Charles pointed out the small whitewashed inn where the Duke of Wellington had established his headquarters. I was surprised to see a familiar figure lounging near the door. He at once knocked out his pipe and came over to our carriage, which had halted in order to give the occupants a better view.

'Mr Fox!' exclaimed Lady Silbury, rather disapprovingly.

I fancied that now she had paid him off she wanted nothing more to do with him; his presence reminded her of the whole sad business which had led to her employing him in the first place.

'Good morning, ladies; I'd heard you were coming here. I've been several times. There are two characters in the vicinity who are up to no good and I've been keeping an eye on them. Miss Aston, I must have a private word with you when it's convenient. I've found out one of the things you wanted to know. Perhaps not quite what you hoped to hear.'

'You may see me at the hotel tomorrow morning,' I told him.

He bowed and backed away.

'What was all that about?' enquired Carrie.

'He's undertaken a small investigation for me. I thought I'd make use of his services while he's here. It's nothing that would interest you.'

'He seems a decent enough man,' pronounced Lady Silbury. 'He was highly recommended to me by a friend, and, like you, undertook a small investigation for me. One can't trust foreigners and it's so convenient having him here.'

At that point a number of local people came up offering cuirasses, bayonets, swords and shako plates for sale. We shook them off with some difficulty and drove on a couple of miles to the village of Mont St Jean and so to the field of battle. Here, at the crossroads, the two carriages stopped and the whole party descended.

'Here was *our* division!' cried Charles with an expansive gesture of his good hand, pointing out the ground occupied by the left wing. 'Behind the road there and in front of that ragged hedge. That's where poor Picton got his discharge. The Union Brigade charged down that slope. Now come and see my famous sandpit! Mind your shoes, ladies.'

A light breeze carried towards us a smell so vile that I caught my breath and Carrie was taken with a fit of coughing.

'Burial pits,' explained Sir Henry. 'They are all over the field. They threw the dead into great holes, tossed wood on top and set fire to it. Not entirely effective, I'm afraid. Do you ladies wish to go on?'

We all assured him that we did, though I thought Carrie and Lydia both looked rather pale and sickly. Charles, still limping a little, led us across the road to the farm of La Haye Sainte, showing us the broken walls with musket and cannon shot still embedded, and then beyond, to the much scarred elm tree under which the Duke of Wellington had surveyed the field. Lydia picked a few of its tattered and discoloured leaves.

We looked down on the rolling plain towards the French position. The crops were flattened and blackened by the storm of battle, the ground pitted by the explosion of shells and churned up by the passage of wheels and hooves. Everywhere lay the litter of two armies: pieces of uniforms, belts and caps and equipment and thousands of sheets of muddy paper. Carrie picked up one, which proved to be a love letter from a French soldier. It was written simply enough for her to understand and it drew sentimental tears.

A large number of crows were continually circling and descending. Yet nature was already reclaiming the field. Poppies flowered amid the beaten crops.

A loud halloo from Charles caught our attention and we followed where he led.

'I'm not at all sure I like this,' Carrie complained. 'There's a lot of rough walking and the smell is disgusting.'

'What did you expect?' I said unsympathetically. 'This is a battlefield, not a picnic. You were asked to wear stout shoes, and look at them! Ruined already! Listen to Charles and you may learn something.'

'For heaven's sake,' he was declaring, 'don't attribute all the glory to the Guards, magnificent as they were. The Imperial Guard advanced along there! The Guards fired on the front of the column. But it was the flank attack of the 52nd that finally finished 'em off and sent them running for their lives. Now, one *can* trust the 52nd to know what they were about. They were part of *the* division in the Peninsula – along with my own regiment, of course. And I can assure you . . . Old Guard over there . . . Maitland over there . . . Colborne and the 52nd swinging round to the side of the advancing column . . . pas de charge . . . couldn't see a damn thing from my sandpit.'

Charles next suggested we should take the road down to the chateau of Hougoumont, where some of the fiercest fighting had taken place. 'And whatever you do, keep in the middle of the road. Don't go near the ditches at the side.'

'Why not?' enquired Carrie.

'Because you might get a horrid surprise. There are quite a few bodies lying there in an advanced state of decomposition.'

Carrie gave a little squeak and clung to my arm.

'How are my girls?' said a voice behind us.

'Oh, Papa!' cried Carrie. 'I wish I hadn't come. I didn't think it would be like this.'

'Well, it is pretty bad, but you were warned. You've got to put up with it now. I believe there's a garden at the chateau, so you'll be able to get away from the nastiness for a while. I think I'll try to find it.'

We reached Hougoumont in about ten minutes and walked up the sloping path from the gate into the courtyard, surrounded by charred and ruined buildings. Here the devastation was at its worst. In continuous attacks, involving 15,000 men, the French had failed to capture Hougoumont from its 2,000 British defenders. The casualties had been horrific. Shells, cannon shot and a fire, which had spread from a haystack to the farm buildings, had completed the work of destruction. The chateau, which had been no castle but rather a pleasant country house, lay roofless and in ruins. The outbuildings were no more than blackened rubble.

A wretched-looking family appeared from a makeshift hut and the man explained that he had worked on the chateau farm before the battle. He and his wife had lost everything. The gentlemen of the party gave them money, which they accepted with gratitude, and the man offered to show us over the place.

I saw Henry talking to the woman, who held a sickly-looking

baby. He handed her some coins and she at once took something from her apron pocket and pressed it into his palm. He came over to me and said the woman had told him to go into the chapel, which had miraculously been preserved intact. The crucifix, she declared, had prevented the flames from spreading.

'Yes,' I said. 'I heard one of my patients talk of the chapel. Some of the wounded were put in there and they believe the cross preserved their lives. We must see it.'

Carrie and I followed Sir Henry toward the chapel and Charles came out as we approached, accompanied by Lady Silbury, who was pale and tight-lipped, and Lydia, who was sobbing into her handkerchief. Charles looked flustered.

'Strange thing,' he said, 'there's something about the place. I don't know what it is, but it's upset the ladies.'

'It has that effect on people,' said the man from the hut.

Sir Henry ushered Carrie and me into the chapel. It was very small, no more than ten feet by ten feet, with a brick floor and whitewashed walls. A little altar bore a statue of the Virgin and Child, and above the door hung a large carved crucifix of polished golden-brown wood, the legs burnt off into charred stumps. The atmosphere overwhelmed me and I could not speak or move. Carrie stifled a sob.

'I can't stand it. This place is haunted!'

She fled, leaving me alone with Sir Henry Croft for the first time since that unexpected display of passion in my room. We both stood very still without speaking for some time. Then he addressed me in a whisper.

'Do you feel you are standing on holy ground?' was his rather curious question.

'Yes. It's not haunted by ghosts, but by a Presence: very calm, very sad and sorrowing.'

'I feel it too. I think the poor souls who were lying here were aware of it.'

He took me by the hand and led me out into the open air. We were immediately confronted by an hysterical scene with two weeping women.

'Poor innocent little creature!' sobbed Lydia Silbury.

'It was horrid! A nightmare! I'll dream of it for the rest of my life!' shrieked Carrie.

'Oh, come now,' said Charles soothingly. 'You mustn't take on so because an emaciated gentleman tried to shake hands with you.'

It appeared Carrie had been frightened by a blackened hand and arm, almost reduced to a skeleton, sticking out of a shallow grave.

'You are heartless, quite heartless,' cried Carrie. 'How can you make jokes about it? Where's Papa? I want to go home.'

'You can't go home till the rest of us do,' Charles said, quite reasonably.

'Pull yourself together, you silly child!' Lady Silbury admonished her severely before turning on her daughter. 'Lydia, stop snivelling!' It transpired that she was weeping over the remains of a dead calf she had seen in a burnt outhouse.

'I think we'll look for some peace and quiet,' said Sir Henry, and I willingly let him lead me into the garden of the chateau.

It was as though our last encounter had never happened, but I felt sure it marked a barrier between us that must never be crossed again.

We suddenly seemed to enter the normal world. One moment we were surrounded by blackened stones, charred wood, ruin, filth and misery, the smell of corruption and burning and the caw of scavenging rooks. Now we found ourselves walking down a turf-covered path overhung with great masses of honeysuckle. The flower beds were in full bloom and a blackbird sang in an orange tree. Some of the yew and holly hedges were torn and ragged and the enclosing wall was loopholed, but compared with what we had seen outside this was a blissful respite from horror.

'I have something for you,' he said. 'Hold out your hand.'

He presented me with the cross of the Legion of Honour.

'Oh, thank you! I'll always keep it in memory of this day. The woman with the baby gave it to you, didn't she?'

He nodded. 'You deserve it more than anyone.'

'Isn't it the custom,' I said, daringly, 'to kiss the recipient on both cheeks?'

'I believe so. There!' He kissed me without embarrassment, his lips merely brushing my face.

'I daresay Bonaparte does it better,' he said, 'but he rather went in for that sort of thing so he has had plenty of practice.'

'*Merci, monsieur!* Would you pick me a small sprig of honeysuckle? I can't quite reach it. Oh no, you needn't, there's some here hanging almost to the ground.'

I ran forward and stumbled over a pair of feet. I withdrew in horror, almost expecting to see a blackened corpse in a ragged uniform, but the boots looked quite new. Sir Henry pulled back the mass of trailing blossom to reveal my Uncle Nat, stretched full length at the side of the path, his eyes shut and exhibiting no sign of life.

CHAPTER TWENTY

'He's dead!' I cried, aghast, only conscious of the fact that I loved Uncle Nat like a father.

'No, he's still breathing,' Sir Henry assured me. 'I can feel his pulse. It looks to me as though he's fainted. It's all this walking over rough ground in the heat and the foul smells.'

I brought out my smelling salts and held them to my uncle's nose. Sir Henry loosened his neckcloth and presently my uncle opened his eyes.

'What am I doing here? What's happened?' his voice was faint, but clear enough. I tried to raise his head and found my hand contacting something warm and sticky. There was a bleeding contusion on the back of his scalp. I wondered at first if he had fainted, as Sir Henry suggested, but the path was covered in turf and there were no stones or hard surfaces where he was lying.

We propped him up as well as we could and I indicated the injury to my companion without saying anything.

'My head hurts,' murmured Uncle Nat, putting up his hand to find the source of the pain.

I looked again. 'You've banged your head,' I told him. 'It isn't very deep, so I don't think it's very serious, but we must wash the wound and ask Mr Kean to have a look at it.'

My uncle could remember nothing of the events immediately preceding his injury. He was strolling peacefully along the garden paths enjoying the scent of the flowers instead of the foul miasma beyond when . . . That was all.

Sir Henry left me with Uncle Nat and ran to fetch help. Presently he returned with Mr Kean, who, as I expected, was quick and efficient in his assessment of the damage.

'How many fingers?' he enquired, holding out his hand in front of my uncle's face.

'Three, of course. D'you think I can't count?'

'Good! Now you must tell me if anything seems blurred. I think you are concussed, which is why you can remember nothing of the incident. The injury is probably quite painful, but not severe. I have some salve with me which I'll apply when I've washed the wound. I'd better use alcohol as I don't trust the water round here. Let me know at once if you experience a headache. Do you think you can stand up? If so, Sir Henry and I can take you back to the chateau.'

'Wait a minute!' Uncle Nat felt in his pockets. 'My watch – my watch has gone and my bunch of seals – and my money. Thank God it wasn't much.'

'This place is still infested with marauders,' said Mr Kean. 'They come to rob the dead, but they won't hesitate to rob the living too if they can see an opportunity.'

But Uncle Nat had his hand inside his coat, feeling an inner pocket.

'It's gone! ' he cried. 'I can get another watch and the money doesn't matter – it's the— '

He stopped suddenly, as though aware of giving away too much. It was perfectly obvious he had been carrying something else on his person that was too valuable to leave in his room, especially after the Moffat burglary. But what could it have been? He was almost sobbing with anger and distress and I tried to comfort him.

Sir Henry and Mr Kean helped him to his feet and he managed to walk back to the chateau building, where his wound was dressed. Mr Kean had thoughtfully brought with him a few items to treat any minor injuries the party might sustain during a long walk over rough ground covered with the relics of warfare.

The rest of our group were very sympathetic and all agreed that they had seen enough and were ready to return home as soon as possible. My uncle was a robust man of little more than fifty, and after a short rest he announced he was quite capable of walking back if he had an arm to lean on.

'There are a couple of rogues over there!' cried Charles, peering through his telescope. We had just emerged from the trees and could now see some distance over the plain. 'I wonder if those two have anything to do with the attack on Mr Wakefield,' Charles continued. 'Halloo!' he bellowed, drawing a pistol from his sash and flourishing it above his head. 'Come here, you blackguards, or I'll shoot you!'

The two hesitated. Until now they had been completely preoccupied with something on the ground at their feet. They took a few steps as though considering whether to run away, and then, perhaps realising flight might be delayed by the uneven, littered character of the ground, they came towards Charles. As they approached I realised it was Mr Moffat and his travel companion, Bowles, who, as usual, carried his enormous satchel.

'What were you doing?' demanded Charles. 'I know you, Moffat – a rogue if ever there was one. I thought you'd been sent packing.'

'We're just picking up a few souvenirs,' whined Bowles. 'I expect you good people have been doing the same.'

'What sort of souvenirs?'

Moffat took a few items from his pocket: a cross of the Legion of Honour, such as I had been given, a shako plate, musket balls and cockades. I wondered if he was planning to sell them to finance his journey home.

'You now! ' snapped Charles. 'Open that satchel – tip out the contents! '

'But they'll be difficult to pick up.'

'Empty it!'

The satchel disgorged its contents on to the ground. There were a few items such as Moffat had already revealed. There were also a pair of pliers and a mass of teeth, torn from the jaws of the young men who had perished.

Moffat looked as though he wished himself anywhere but here. Bowles, however, was quite unabashed.

'My employer', he said, 'is in the highest rank of London

dentists. He sent me here specifically to collect teeth from healthy specimens who had no further use for them. He can charge a patient 200 guineas for a good set. I'm only supplying a need.'

'It's disgusting!' Carrie turned away in horror.

'It's more than disgusting!' cried Charles. 'D'you think we endured all this for our dead to be desecrated by scum like you? The humblest private solder is worth a hundred of you?'

'Not much now, in the way of pickings,' grumbled Bowles. 'It was best in the first few days, but the more that were buried the fewer I had to go at. But there are still a few to be had if you know where to look. They fill the pits right up to the top, so you can often find a likely client in the uppermost layer of corpses.'

'This isn't the largest part of the haul!' Charles was flushed with indignation. 'The rest must be back in your room.'

'But they're no use to you, sir,' whined Bowles. 'They're no use to anyone except my master and his patients.'

'Leave him,' said Sir Henry quietly. 'I've heard of this. Hyenas and vultures always benefit from death. Get off, the pair of you, before my brother carries out his threat to shoot you.'

'If I had the use of both my hands I'd strangle him!'

'Clear off, and if you aren't packed up and out of the hotel before nightfall I'll see you're thrown out,' Sir Henry concluded.

Suddenly Mr Kean, who had been standing a little way back, strode forward, pushing between the two Crofts, and dealt Bowles a blow across the face, which sent him staggering backwards. He said something to him in a low voice, but I could not make out the words – which is probably just as well, because I imagine they were obscene.

'That's all his sort understands,' he said abruptly. 'You gentlemen are too lenient.'

Moffat had already taken off as fast as he could and Bowles stumbled after him, clutching the side of his face.

Charles kicked some soil over the contents of Bowles' satchel, and I pulled up some forget-me-nots and placed them on top. He looked at me gratefully.

'I'm glad you understand,' he said.

We walked back in a sober mood, my uncle supported by

Mr Kean and Sir Henry. Carrie and I followed behind. Lady Silbury and her daughter had gone ahead of us.

'Do you think those horrid men attacked Papa?' Carrie shivered although the afternoon was very warm. 'That Moffat makes me feel sick. He's capable of anything. Perhaps he attacked Papa in revenge for being found out.'

'More likely to gather funds for his return to England,' I said, but I'm not at all sure he was responsible.'

'He should have been searched. Who knows what was hidden in his pockets?'

'If he was guilty,' I suggested, 'wouldn't he have tried to get as far away as possible?'

'I don't trust him an inch.'

Charles caught up with us, limping rather more heavily than when we started. We were heading back along the road to Mont St Jean, near which our carriages were waiting.

'It's not too far,' he assured us. 'It's a small battlefield after all. That's why the casualties were so heavy. We were all packed close together – nearly 200,000 in a mile and a half, to say nothing of horses and artillery. They say the Duke was in tears when he heard the extent of the casualties. He never wasted lives if he could help it, and he risked his own more than anyone in the field. It was a miracle he escaped unhurt. He was everywhere at once – wherever the greatest danger threatened.'

'Mama will be interested to hear that,' said Carrie. 'He's quite a hero of hers.'

When we reached Mont St Jean we decided to take some refreshment at the inn. I do not think any of us could even think of food while on the actual battlefield with all its horrors, but now we were confronted with a simple meal of brown bread, butter and cheese washed down with weak beer and wine, we all tucked in with a good appetite – even my uncle, who was looking much restored.

We climbed in our carriages rather wearily and for a time sat in silence. Lady Silbury fanned herself and declared she never wanted to visit another battlefield as long as she lived. Then she suddenly broached the subject of Ben.

'Have you heard from your brother, Miss Wakefield?' she enquired of Carrie.

'No, but he's never been a very good correspondent and the army has been continually on the move. They seem to be in a different place nearly every day, so it must be difficult to communicate.'

'I suppose so.'

'We are sure to hear when they reach Paris,' added Carrie, 'and that should be any time now.'

'Doesn't that depend on Bonaparte?' Lydia looked troubled. 'Suppose there's another battle?'

'He's abdicated,' I said, 'so he's unlikely to gather another army and the best of what he had has been destroyed.'

'Let's hope so,' said Lady Silbury. 'I'll be glad when we get home. I don't think we'll ever go abroad again.'

'Mama, I thought we were going to take a little tour of the Low Countries and then go on to Paris,' Lydia protested.

'I suppose you were hoping to see Lieutenant Wakefield again. You can forget that, my dear.'

'But why? I thought you liked him.'

'Liking does not make him eligible and he has not been honest with us. The unfortunate gentleman in the other carriage who was so disgracefully robbed is his father. Your father too, Miss Wakefield. Your brother told me he owned an estate called Summer Hill in Warwickshire.'

'Summer Hill is a street in Birmingham,' I said. 'It is on the outskirts of the town near the jewellery quarter. We are about to move to Bath, where my uncle is opening a shop.'

'A shop!' Lady Silbury scarcely suppressed a shudder. 'I suspected Lieutenant Wakefield exaggerated, but it was more than that. He told us a pack of lies.'

I glanced at Lydia, who was sitting with bowed head, her hands clenched in her lap.

'A jeweller from Birmingham!' Lady Silbury groaned. 'Surely he wasn't stupid enough to suppose we'd never find out. You two young ladies have done very well to rise above your background. As for you, Lydia, you've had a lucky escape. The sooner I get you home, the better.'

Lydia was not, I felt, a rebel by nature. She would accept her mother's judgement and eventually marry a suitable young aristocrat, but she would keep Ben's diamonds and his last note in a secret compartment of her jewel box or writing desk. The affair could not have gone very far or very deep, but she would always remember the young soldier who was her first love.

I was sure by now that Ben was dead. Mr Fox was coming to bring me the news tomorrow. His expressionless tone of voice had told me all I needed to know and it was no more than I expected.

That, with the gloom and horror of the battlefield, made me profoundly depressed, and I could not help but feel there was worse to come.

CHAPTER TWENTY-ONE

Fox was as good as his word and came round to the Hôtel Britannique the following morning. Carrie had gone down to sit with her mother, so I received him in my room.

I unlocked the door and we both entered. He placed a chair for me near the door and stood a little way inside the room until I begged him to sit down, when he perched awkwardly on the edge of the bed.

'I'm glad I'm able to speak to you privately, Miss Aston,' he began. 'I am going to say things that I don't think either of us would care for others to hear at present. Firstly, I am sorry to tell you that your cousin, Lieutenant Wakefield, did not rejoin his regiment. As far as they're concerned, he's missing. I only hope they don't brand him a deserter.'

'It's no more than I expected,' I said. 'I suppose the red-haired young officer poor Paddy saw was my cousin.'

'And it sounds as though someone put an end to his life by violent means.'

'You mean murder?'

He nodded.

'But who can have done such a thing?' I demanded. 'And why?'

'Most murders are carried out for gain: money or freedom or revenge. I think your cousin had something in his possession that was valuable enough to be killed for.'

'Diamonds? I didn't tell you, but he left a note for Lydia Silbury with a piece broken off a larger piece of jewellery. It looked like part of a necklace.'

'Ah, that explains it. Let us suppose your cousin came upon a diamond necklace on the battlefield after the conclusion of the action. Probably the next day.'

'Loot?'

'I don't suppose he thought of it that way. Soldiers have always helped themselves to the enemy's possessions. I believe there was a veritable orgy of looting after the battle of Vittoria, when the French abandoned their baggage train. One of the regiments still has King Joseph's silver chamber pot.'

'So someone must have found out what he had and killed him for it?'

'But by then he had handed it over to his father, who is a jeweller. He'd be able to break it up, reset the stones and make a huge profit.'

'Before you go any further, Mr Fox, I must tell you what happened to my uncle yesterday, while we were visiting Hougoumont.'

I hastily explained how we had found Uncle Nat lying unconscious in the garden with a head wound and how he searched his pockets in a panic and seemed very distressed when he found an item missing.

'It wasn't his watch or money, so it must have been the necklace, but he wouldn't say what it was. Do you suppose it was stolen by the man who murdered his son?'

'It sounds all too likely, but this gives me an idea. Before I do anything I'd like you to have a quiet word with your uncle. You'll have to break the news of his son's death, which is difficult enough, but you seem to be a resourceful and tactful young lady. You'll do it as well as anyone. Then perhaps you can get more information out of him. He'll want to know who was responsible for the young man's murder. I've got a pretty good idea myself, but I need further proof. I'll let you know when I've got it.'

'There's one more detail which I've just remembered,' I told him. 'My aunt said that when Ben called to see them on the night of the 19th he spent a while talking to my uncle on the landing. Now, when Moffat and Bowles came to the hotel I heard them talking in a window alcove as I came upstairs. I didn't come near enough to hear what they were saying because they heard my footsteps and fell silent. Now, if someone came up very quietly he could have listened to the conversation between my uncle and Ben and found out about the necklace.'

'Yes, I'm sure you're right, but you must get your uncle to tell as much as he knows. We can't progress any further until you've got that out of the way.'

'He has no memory of the attack. Mr Kean thinks he was hit with a stone or possibly a piece of wood.'

'Yes, I daresay, but you go and see your uncle now. I have further business in this hotel so I may still be here later today and I may have more news for you.'

I thanked him for his efforts and paid him for his work so far, engaging his services for another week. Then I went to see Aunt Hetty and Uncle Nat and suggested to him a quiet walk in the park if he felt up to it.

'Last night I had a headache,' he said, 'and your aunt advised me to take a dose of laudanum, so I did, and I slept well and feel much better this morning. But a little fresh air will do me good, especially after those foul smells yesterday. I began to feel as though I'd never breathe clean air again.'

We walked at an easy pace until we reached the park, where we soon found an empty bench.

My uncle sighed. 'This was such a happy place, so full of life. Everywhere seems to be in mourning.'

'Uncle,' I began, 'what do you suppose happened to Ben after he parted from you the last time?'

'He went back to say goodbye to his mother. Then he left us. He was supposed to be rejoining his regiment. They'd been ordered to proceed to Nivelles on the 19th to wait for the Duke to join them, which he did the next day. Ben had a horse, so he'd be able to get to Nivelles in time to join the march to the French border.'

'But you haven't heard from him since?'

'No, of course not. I'd have told you. It must be very difficult for them to send letters when they're on the move.'

'It probably is, but I must tell you, Uncle, that someone I

know carried out an investigation for me. He found a courier taking dispatches to the Duke of Wellington and he agreed to pass an enquiry to Ben's regiment. Ben never rejoined it. He has disappeared.'

'*What?*'

'The person who found this out for me was Mr Fox.'

'The Bow Street officer who rescued Carrie?'

'Yes, and I'm sure he's completely reliable. But there is more. I would not have told you if I hadn't expected foul play, but if I am to be honest with you, dear Uncle Nat, I beg you to be honest with me.'

I told him of the story related by poor dead Paddy and how Fox had tracked down the men who had taken the red-haired officer for burial.

My uncle went very pale and his hands trembled. 'This can't be true.'

'Then where is he? Why has he not got in touch with you?'

He shook his head sadly.

'I must know, Uncle, what it was you had stolen from you yesterday. I'm sure it was something Ben passed on to you and for which he was killed. There's a section missing which I've seen in the possession of Lydia Silbury. Was it a diamond necklace?'

'Oh, my God!'

'I see I have guessed correctly, so I might as well know the rest.' I put my hands over his reassuringly.

He then told me the whole story. The day after the battle Ben had been approached by a Prussian trooper. This man explained, in fractured English, that he had been among those who had captured the Emperor Napoleon's travelling carriage at Genappe. Bonaparte had been unable to return to it after the battle and had escaped on horseback.

The carriage was full of valuables, which were shared out among the men. Some were handed over to their officers, but many items were kept as loot. Concealed inside the lining of the carriage was a diamond necklace and this the trooper had pocketed before being sent to the rear with a minor wound.

Ben gave the Prussian five napoleons for the necklace and decided to bring it to his father for safekeeping.

'He knew I'd be able to make use of it and share the profits with him. It wasn't stealing, was it? Bonaparte can hardly lay claim to it now and it doesn't belong to anyone else. I reckoned it was worth between £25,000 and £30,000.'

'As much as that?' I hardly knew what else to say as there was some truth in what he said.

'I suppose Ben should have stayed where he was,' Uncle Nat continued ruefully, 'but there was such chaos after the battle and so much coming and going he didn't think anyone would miss him for a few hours. He tied a bandage round his head in case anyone questioned his presence in Brussels.'

'We must tell Mr Fox the whole story. He says he thinks he knows who killed Ben, but he must have proof.'

To my horror my uncle leaned forward, resting elbows on knees, and began weeping. I put my arm around his shoulders. There were not many people about and Brussels was used to signs of grief. He was just another parent mourning a son lost in battle. It would have been so much better had that been so. The sorrow would still be as great, but the shame surrounding this particular death made it harder to bear.

'I don't know how we'll tell your aunt,' sobbed poor Uncle Nat. 'It will kill her.'

'We can't keep it from her forever. She'll find out eventually. It's better if it comes from us.'

My uncle was not normally a man who showed his feelings. I had never seen him so distraught.

'He died because of that – that *bauble*! It would have been better if he had been killed in battle like so many others. At least I could have felt proud of him. He'd have died for *something*. Now I can only feel shame as well as loss. I'm glad the thing was stolen. I never want to see it again.'

Aunt Hetty would remain in blissful ignorance for a little while longer. My uncle was right; the news of Ben's death could kill her, or at least turn her entire life into a desert so that no brightness or pleasure could ever relieve the pain. Uncle Nat had never loved Ben as much as she did; Carrie was always his favourite. He would recover eventually; he had his work and his daughter. Aunt Hetty had nothing.

On our return to the hotel we found Mr Fox waiting.

'Ah, I see you know, sir. My condolences,' he said, on seeing my uncle's downcast demeanour.

'You must find him – you must find out who did it?' Uncle Nat begged him.

'I think I already have, but first, sir, perhaps you'd take a look at these items. Number one –'

He held out a handsome gold watch, turning it round to reveal the monogram on the back.

'That's *my* watch!' exclaimed my uncle. 'How did you come by it? Surely it wasn't you?'

'Of course not. Please look at item number two.' He held up a bunch of seals. 'Your initials are on one and a classical head on an onyx and—'

'Yes, yes, they are mine.'

'And this purse containing £5 worth of coins?'

'Yes, my daughter netted it for me.'

'I must return these things to where I found them. They are proof of who attacked you yesterday and I don't yet want the thief to find out that I know of his guilt. You will get them back later, I assure you.'

'They don't matter much.'

'They were taken to hide the removal of something much more important. Like you, he carries this item on his person – at least, there's no sign of it in his room. I'll put these things back exactly where I found them. I will soon reveal the perpetrator of these crimes, but I've one or two other matters to check first. May I see you later, Miss Aston?'

'Yes, of course.'

Mr Fox took off at a brisk pace for the staircase.

'What was all that about?' enquired my uncle.

'I'm sure he'll tell us everything quite soon, but I think he wants to hear from me how you came by the necklace. I don't think he cares to trouble you at present. You've gone through enough.'

'And more to come.'

'Carrie will be upset as well as Aunt Hetty. Would you like me to tell her?'

'Carrie's feelings are mainly on the surface,' he said, with some astuteness. 'She's never had that much to do with Ben and there's six years' difference. She'll cry a lot, of course. Better tell her and her mother at the same time, but not just yet.'

'I'll walk up with you and see if I can find out where Fox has gone. He's very close; he won't reveal anything until he's got all the information in place.'

I left my uncle at the door of his room, parting with an affectionate kiss.

When I reached the third floor I encountered Charles Croft on his way down. He hailed me with undisguised pleasure.

'There you are!' he cried. 'I was hoping to see you earlier, but you must have gone out.'

'I went for a walk with my uncle.'

'I hope you weren't too tired after your exertions yesterday, especially your poor uncle. Is he quite recovered?'

'He seems to be. Are you going out?'

'I breakfasted late this morning. I must admit I was rather knocked up yesterday, though not as badly as on my previous visit. Henry fusses over me like an old woman and he insisted I must rest today. He's gone out visiting one of the hospitals. I'm just going to look for him.' He was about to go on his way when he seemed to recall something. 'Oh, by the bye, you remember you once asked me what croakers were, in army parlance?'

'Yes, you said they were people who complained, which is what I supposed.'

'And quite right too. But there's another use for the expression which I didn't mention at the time. I think we were interrupted by Lydia Silbury.'

'And what is it?'

'A croaker – or crocus – is a surgeon.'

CHAPTER TWENTY-TWO

Charles went cheerfully on his way, quite unaware of the shock he had given me. I stood outside my door in a daze and there I was found by Mr Fox, on his way down from the attic rooms where the poorer guests were accommodated.

'Miss Aston!' he hailed me. 'I hoped I might find you. I've been returning your uncle's watch and seals to the place I found them. I used my skeleton key, of course – easy enough on simple locks like these.'

'I know which room you visited,' I told him.

'Really? Do you mind if we go inside for a few minutes? I wouldn't like us to be overheard.'

We entered my room as on the previous occasion and sat down to exchange confidences.

I told him what Charles Croft had told me, and how it explained Paddy's words, which had seemed so mysterious at the time.

'Mr Kean has been going down in the night to visit the wounded,' I said. 'He could have heard my uncle and cousin talking on the landing, then he waited for Ben to come out after saying goodbye to his mother and attacked him on the stairs. I suppose he thought he still carried the necklace. My uncle told me it was looted from Bonaparte's carriage by a Prussian soldier, who sold it to Ben for five napoleons.'

'Ah, I suspected as much. Our friend has it on him now; he won't risk leaving it anywhere. It must be worth thousands. Your uncle would know, of course. He must have taken charge of the necklace and been robbed of it in the garden at Hougoumont.'

146

'There's something else,' I said, 'something I noticed a while ago but I was too preoccupied with my work in the courtyard to make the connection. I saw Kean take off his coat and roll up his sleeves. The cuffs of his shirt were very neatly mended and I thought of that poor woman Carrie and I found in the park. It seems a hundred years ago now. Her cheap cotton gloves were very neatly darned. There may be nothing in it at all, but . . .'

'Only a woman would notice something of that sort. You are very observant.'

'I still can't understand Mr Kean. He's worked like a slave for no reward.'

'I expect he thought he might get taken on by the army, but since the great victory the war is coming to an end. The army will need fewer surgeons, not more.'

'Yet I don't think that was his only motive. He really was dedicated to saving the lives of those poor men. How can someone who did so much good do so much evil?'

'It does happen, more often than you'd think. But that woman you found was his wife. He'd abandoned her when he was thrown out of the navy. They had a child, which she left with her mother while she came looking for him. I found letters from him in the pocket of her pelisse. He was in such a hurry to hide the body that he must have overlooked them, which was careless of him.'

'Did he tell you why they threw him out of the navy?' he asked.

'Yes,' I said, 'he told me he had to amputate the Captain's arm, and it resulted in his death. The Captain had friends in high places who had him removed, even though the Captain would have died anyway. He seemed very bitter about it.'

'Oh yes, he would! I had the true story from his wife. She said he was a heavy drinker and was drunk when he performed the operation.'

'I don't think he drinks now. I remember the Crofts offered him brandy after he operated on Charles's hand, but he wouldn't take it. I've never seen him the worse for drink.'

'I'm sure you haven't. But he must have seen possession

of that necklace as the solution to all his problems. He could have lived in comfort for the rest of his life on the proceeds. As he'd done one murder he wouldn't have any scruples about committing another. His wife said he was a violent man, but she seemed devoted to him.'

'Obviously he didn't feel the same about her.'

'He's an awkward customer and I fancy he may be dangerous if confronted with his crimes. I think we've got enough evidence, but being in a foreign country makes things difficult. I'd like to force a confession from him, but I'm not sure how it is to be done. Meanwhile, say nothing, not even to your uncle. If Kean speaks to you, try to answer him normally. At least you don't have to work with him any more.'

I shook my head. 'He's saved so many lives. Was it to make amends, do you suppose?'

'If it was then it didn't stop him attacking your uncle and afterwards treating the injury as though it was nothing to do with him.'

'You ran a great risk going into his room.'

'Ah, but I knew he was out. He's been visiting some of his former patients in their billets.'

'I really believe he cares for them.'

'Professional pride perhaps.'

'Perhaps. But he's a strange mixture. I don't understand him at all.'

'He probably doesn't understand himself, but we're not in the business of sorting out his character, only of proving his guilt. Remember, Miss Aston, keep all this to yourself.'

I nodded and went down to my aunt and uncle's room, where, to my confusion, I found Mr Kean. He smiled and nodded towards me by way of greeting.

'I thought I'd drop in on my way back from this morning's visits,' he explained. 'I wanted to see how my only lady patient was doing. She should be back on her feet quite soon as she's been doing well on crutches. And your uncle seems to have got over that nasty blow on the head.'

'It's been very tedious!' exclaimed Aunt Hetty. 'There's been so much going on and I've been unable to see anything for myself.'

Mr Kean suddenly directed a searching look in my direction. I hoped I showed no embarrassment and I tried to smile. He took his leave and Carrie added her praises to those of her parents.

'Such a good man!' she said. 'Rather abrupt in his manner, but that's only to be expected after all those years at sea. You know better than anyone, Lizzie, how much good he has done.'

'Yes,' I agreed, 'he's a very skilful surgeon.' I hoped my expression was not giving anything away.

I made my excuses and left. Although I had no idea what I was going to do I was too restless and agitated to stay with my family.

As I approached the landing near my room I heard some curious noises: grunts and thumps and a flood of colourful language. The two participants were at first quite unaware of my approach and I was momentarily so bewildered I could not make out what was going on save that I found myself looking at the bald spot on top of Mr Fox's head, which I had never seen before.

He was lying flat on his back in the passage, being pummelled by Anthony Kean. The law officer was the taller and probably the more agile of the two, but Kean was built like a bull and seemed to be made of muscle, with broad shoulders and a barrel chest. He was clearly getting the better of his opponent, kneeling on top of him and holding him by the throat with one hand while trying to wrest a pistol from his grip with the other.

'Stop that! ' I screamed, quite ineffectually. They were unlikely to take any notice of me.

Kean landed a blow on Fox's jaw and suddenly leapt over to me, seized my wrist in an iron grip and flung open the door of my room, which I had forgotten to lock.

'You'll make a good hostage,' he said. He dragged me into the room despite my struggles and pressed the muzzle of the pistol against my head. 'Now keep quiet and do as I tell you!'

He slammed the door and locked it.

CHAPTER TWENTY-THREE

Kean almost threw me into the armchair and then sat opposite to me on the edge of the bed.

'Now we are settled we can have a talk,' he said, bringing out a handkerchief and dabbing his bleeding lip. 'But don't try to play any tricks on me – they won't work and may make me lose my temper as that interfering Fox did. You are my prisoner and I intend to use you for bargaining purposes.'

I was terrified and did not trust myself to speak immediately, but I realised my only chance was to make him talk for as long as possible. I hoped Fox was not so badly hurt that he could not summon help. Someone would eventually find him lying in the passage, but how long would it be before that happened?

'I think you know more than is good for you?' he said. 'What has Fox told you?'

'Little more than I had already surmised for myself. I suppose you know Carrie and I found the body of your wife in the park?'

'A tiresome woman! Whining, clinging and complaining! It was like having an anchor chained to my leg. I was a fool ever to have married her. I should have chosen a girl like you – someone with courage and spirit.'

'You have a child. Surely—'

'A miserable grizzling boy. He takes after his mother. I can't see any of myself in him. In fact, if she hadn't been such a cold fish I might have suspected something. But no, I fathered him unfortunately.'

'And you don't care what becomes of him?'

'Not really. I was away at sea so much that I was never concerned about domestic matters.'

I listened, but could hear nothing from outside.

'How did you come to kill my cousin Ben?' I enquired.

'You weren't particularly attached to him, were you?'

'No, we never got on.'

'Then you won't waste many tears on him.'

'No, but his parents will. You've ruined their lives.'

He shrugged. 'I don't really know them. Your aunt is rather silly and your uncle a dull, worthy burgher.'

'But Ben—'

'Since you are interested and we have some time to kill I will tell you. I was in the habit of going down to the courtyard in the middle of the night to see how my patients were faring.'

'Yes, I know, and it was an admirable thing to do.'

'Who cares? I carried my shoes in my hand to avoid disturbing the other residents. On returning to my room on the night of the 19th I heard your uncle and his son talking on the landing nearest to his room. They didn't hear me and although I didn't catch every word they were saying I heard enough to know they were in possession of a diamond necklace looted on the battlefield. I waited until I heard them go back into the bedroom. After a few minutes your cousin Ben came out on his own. I saw him winding a bandage round his head. At that point I made my presence known. I asked him what he was doing, reminded him that I was a surgeon and asked to see his wound. Of course, I was sure there was no such injury. This led to a struggle and he fell backwards down the steps, cracking his head in the process. When I got to him he was dead. It must have been instantaneous and it *was* accidental. You have my word on that. I debated what to do and eventually decided that the simplest way of dealing with the problem was to take him downstairs and put him in the courtyard with the wounded.'

'I heard a different story from the soldier who lay next to Ben. He said his throat had been cut, which suggests he was knocked unconscious by the fall and you finished off the job with a scalpel.'

A look of faint surprise crossed his face momentarily and then he smiled.

'I believe the solder in question is dead, so what evidence is there?'

'It is known where Ben is buried. If he was to be disinterred his injuries would be discovered and you might find yourself involved.'

'But I'll be far away by then. I have you as a hostage, remember?'

'Did you think Ben had the necklace on him?'

'It was a possibility, but after a search I realised he must have handed it over to his father. I had to make sure he wouldn't recover and identify me as his assailant, but he could well have died from that head injury.'

'That didn't stop you from attacking my poor uncle – striking him from behind.'

'I didn't want him to see me, did I?'

'So you've got the necklace?'

There was a pause as we both became conscious of sounds in the corridor outside: footsteps and hushed voices.

'Oh yes,' he said. 'I have the necklace. I didn't want his watch and purse – they are paltry indeed compared with this beauty – but I had to make it look like a common robbery.'

He brought out a glittering cascade of diamonds.

'There's a section missing,' I said. 'Do you know why?'

'No, I don't. I suppose you do.'

'Oh yes. It's nice to know I have some information you don't possess.'

'I thought it was damage acquired during its rough treatment after the battle, or perhaps the Prussian had broken off a piece as a souvenir.'

'No, Ben left it for Lydia Silbury at the Hôtel Belle Vue.'

'She's welcome to it. It'll have to be broken up anyway, which is a pity.'

Again we heard low masculine voices and a scraping at the lock.

'You can stop that scratching with your skeleton keys!'

yelled Kean, so loudly that he startled me. 'If you try to enter I'll shoot Miss Aston.'

'Elizabeth!' I recognised Henry Croft's voice. 'Are you all right?'

'Perfectly!' I shouted back. 'He hasn't hurt me, but he's pointing a pistol at me. Don't do anything rash.'

'Very sensible advice,' said Kean.

'How long are we going to sit here? Are we going to die of hunger and thirst? You'll fall asleep eventually and you'll drop the pistol and my friends will break in and—'

'So you hope. Here, put it on!' He suddenly threw the necklace into my lap.

'But why?'

'It was meant to encircle the neck of a beautiful woman. I want to see it in its rightful place.' With trembling hands I fastened the necklace and adjusted it so that it lay evenly.

'Yes,' he sighed, 'that's how it should be. Beauty deserves beauty.'

He raised the pistol and levelled it at me, or so I thought. I closed my eyes tightly and tried to pray. There was a deafening explosion and the acrid reek of gunpowder. For a few bewildered seconds I thought I had been shot and then the door crashed open and I was caught up in a strong pair of arms.

'Don't look, Elizabeth – keep your eyes shut.'

I was lifted out of my chair and hastened out of the room into the passage. Henry Croft propped me against the wall, holding me very close as my legs were giving way.

'Thank God you're unhurt, my poor brave girl. How dare he!' He smothered my face and neck with kisses.

'What happened?' I asked. 'Did he miss?'

'No, he turned the pistol on himself. That's why I told you to close your eyes. Oh, God, what shall we do? I can't bear to let you go!'

Mr Fox and Charles were in the room. I suppose both of them were well used to seeing the victims of gunshots and when they emerged neither seemed much disconcerted by the gory scene they had witnessed.

'Suicide,' said Fox. 'No point in accusing him now. It saves the hangman a job. I suppose he realised that taking you hostage wasn't going to succeed. You're wearing the necklace, Miss Aston.'

'He asked me to put it on.' I struggled with trembling fingers to undo the catch.

'Let me,' said Henry, dexterously unfastening the diamond clasps and gently caressing the back of my neck as he did so.

'At least it's brought you two together,' said Charles with a grin.

'Are we?'

I looked into Henry Croft's face and saw his expression change to something like anguish.

'I think', I told him, 'we must have a serious conversation. Not now, but quite soon. I deserve an explanation. I have not endured all this for nothing.'

'Of course not, but—'

'Oh, stop butting buts!' said Charles. 'I don't know what's the matter with you. If I had Miss Aston in my arms I'd think myself the luckiest fellow on earth.'

'And so I do,' Henry sighed. 'It's not as easy as you suppose. Besides, there's much to do now. The Belgian authorities must be informed and Kean's remains removed. Miss Aston and her cousin can no longer occupy this room, so their belongings must be transferred to another.'

'Next door will be empty now the Moffats have gone,' I said. 'I'm sure Madame Dubois will agree. It will be less trouble to move in there.'

'You must be prepared to wait a while,' said Fox. 'This room is in a mess and you can't possibly go inside. We'll see about getting your things later.'

'And your unfortunate aunt and uncle must be told the whole story,' said Henry. 'I've no doubt they'll apply for the exhumation of their son's remains and have him buried in a grave on his own with a suitable monument. He won't be the only officer to lie in Brussels.'

'I'll deal with the authorities,' said Fox. 'They already know me and have a certain respect for Bow Street officers. And we must decide what is to be done with this.' He held aloft the glittering cause of all the trouble.

A long time afterwards we found out the origin of the necklace. It had been given to the Emperor Napoleon by his disreputable sister Pauline, who had a formidable collection of jewellery. He was to use it, she suggested, if ever he needed emergency funds.

We did not know this when confronted with the problem, though it would have made no difference if we had. To whom did the necklace belong? Then we were told that most of the jewels discovered in the imperial carriage had been handed over to Field Marshal Blücher, who passed them on to the King of Prussia to join the crown jewels. That seemed to be an appropriate destination for a necklace that had brought nothing but suffering to all those who possessed it.

CHAPTER TWENTY-FOUR

At first Aunt Hetty refused to believe that Ben was dead.

'No, he can't have been killed. We *saw* him! He came to visit us in the middle of the night the day after the battle. Of course we haven't heard from him; he's never been a good correspondent and he has his military duties to occupy him. They've been on the move all the time. When we go to Paris we shall see him again. I'll be on my feet before then.'

Eventually, after denying everything, she was forced to admit that her darling was no more. She was almost paralysed with shock for some time and profoundly depressed, weeping and moaning, eating little and drinking too much alcohol. Matters improved somewhat when she was able to walk a little, but I think Uncle Nat's prediction was true. She would never get over it. Eventually she convinced herself that Ben died of a wound received in battle which he had bravely concealed. We let her believe it as it seemed to give her some comfort. It meant that Ben could be mourned as hero instead of pitied as the victim of a murderer.

My uncle could not mask his grief with delusions and dutifully made the necessary arrangements for Ben's exhumation and reburial in the Protestant cemetery of St Joost, where many other officers were interred. Aunt Hetty fretted over the design for a monument to go on the grave.

We tried to convince her that ostentation was vulgar, especially as Ben was only one among many thousands of fatalities, but Uncle Nat gave way in the end and a trophy of arms with a flowery inscription was commissioned from a local stonemason. It was explained that graves should be allowed to sink before being burdened with the weight of a monument, but she insisted it had to be in place before she left Brussels.

Carrie went back home with her parents and joined them in a set of rooms above the shop in Bath, which soon prospered as so many rich and fashionable people visited the town. Aunt Hetty told everyone about her beloved son who died as a result of wounds received at Waterloo. She gained much sympathy, which seemed to sustain her.

Uncle Nat was fortunate to have a new business to keep him fully occupied and was pleased when Carrie formed a very suitable attachment to a local attorney who came from a respectable and well-to-do family.

It only remains for me to relate my own fortunes.

Three days after the death of Anthony Kean, when all the questions had been asked and answered and all the horrors cleared away, a normal morning dawned.

At breakfast, which Carrie and I shared with the Croft brothers, I indicated that the time had come for the discussion I had demanded. I was by now desperately in love with Henry Croft and I could not bear to contemplate parting from him. He had given every indication that he returned my feelings, but so far had given no reason for refusing to face the consequences of a declared passion.

I suggested we should go for a walk outside the gates and take coffee at one of the little cafés out there. We could sit at a table in privacy, but be surrounded by cheerful scenes. He seemed ill at ease as though he wished himself elsewhere and seemed to be waiting for me to make the first approach.

'You know why I wish to speak to you,' I began, 'and I may regret it even more if I don't say it. You'll think me very unladylike for being so forward, but I never had any pretensions to gentility. My father was a surgeon and my uncle is a jeweller.'

He said nothing, his face carrying an expression of melancholy that was all too usual with him.

'I must know why you told me marriage between us is

impossible,' I continued. 'You are far from being a snob. I can't believe superior social rank would keep you from someone you truly love. So what is it?'

'Isn't it obvious? I have nothing: an income of £200 a year, a crumbling old house that is falling about my ears – nothing! How could I ask any woman to share my poverty? You have enjoyed every comfort in life: a good education, servants, a pleasant home and pretty clothes. I couldn't subject you to increasing squalor with no hope of improvement. And as for children – how could we contemplate raising a family in such circumstances? Paying for their education, finding them respectable employment . . .'

'Is that all?' I cut in.

'Isn't it enough?'

'No, it isn't. You see, I haven't yet explained my circumstances to you. You know my father was a surgeon. He and my mother died in a tragic accident when I was six; otherwise he was set to rise to the very top of his profession. Even so, he was very successful. No – let me finish.'

He had taken my hand between both of his and held it as though it was something precious that he might lose.

'My father left me over £20,000,' I said.

'Then you are a rich woman,' he sighed. 'I cannot marry you for your money.'

'You've only just discovered I have any.'

'How could I possibly live off my wife's fortune? It's contemptible.'

'Then don't. If you insist we'll have a marriage settlement drawn up whereby I retain control of most of my money. If I spend it on making my life more comfortable by having the roof mended and sending my children to good schools, then so be it. Why should we be kept apart by *money*? If I can't marry you I shall marry no one and devote myself to whatever charitable works are appropriate for an ageing spinster.'

'You'll never be that. You'll find some good man who'll make you happy.'

'But I've already found him and I've no intention of letting him go.'

I think I had convinced him; he raised my hands to his lips and then stood up, drawing me to my feet.

'This place is too public. Let's find somewhere secluded so that I can kiss you.'

'And you promise not to run off muttering nonsense about it being impossible to marry?'

'Oh no, the event can't be too soon for me. I suppose I'll have to ask your uncle's permission.'

'He'll be delighted to give it, but it's only a courtesy. I am twenty-three, after all. We could be married here in Brussels and go on to Paris for our honeymoon.'

'Yes, at least I can pay for *that*! I may be poor, but I'm not a pauper. Charles will be going soon as he's nearly fit for travel. It's strange, but I thought it was Charles you preferred. He certainly likes *you*!'

'At first, perhaps. He taught me to waltz and I found him quite captivating. Then I kissed him goodbye because he asked me and I feared he might be killed. But it didn't count for anything once I'd come to know you.'

'It's a strange love, born of war. I wonder if we ought to be grateful to Napoleon Bonaparte. Without him we'd never have met.'

'Perish the thought!' I exclaimed. 'But I don't think we should be too kindly disposed towards him after the trouble he's caused.'

'Where shall we go?'

'I have an idea. We'll go to the park. I remember Charles saying how a friend of his saw the Duke himself disappear into a little shrubbery with a beautiful blonde lady. I think I know where it is.'

'Then lead on, my love. What is good enough for the Duke is surely good enough for us.'

'I'm not at all sure that this *was* the spot,' I said at last, pushing through the branches of a little copse. I was not greatly concerned as it was a long way from the place where Carrie and I found Kean's wife.

'It doesn't matter,' said Henry. 'It's a fine and private place and that's all that matters.' He threw down his hat and began to untie my bonnet.

'I suppose we'll have to be married by one of the Protestant clergy,' I said, 'unless there's a regimental chaplain. They can't *all* have gone off with the army. We used to attend Mr Stonestreet's services and I know he conducted marriages. Is he still available or did he depart with the Guards?'

'Not another word!' he said, and silenced me with a kiss.